Hogan's Bluff

When his father is killed and his sister kidnapped following a confrontation with a powerful rancher it falls to fourteen-year-old Zachariah Hogan to set matters straight. That this would entail his riding with a band of Sioux warriors was something that the boy could not, in his wildest dreams, ever have imagined. So it is that a youngster who has not yet begun to shave becomes embroiled in the last action of the Great Sioux War of 1876.

Hogan's Bluff

Harriet Cade

A Black Horse Western

ROBERT HALE

ISBN 978-0-7198-2877-5

The Crowood Press
The Stable Block
Crowood Lane
Ramsbury
Marlborough
Wiltshire SN8 2HR

www.bhwesterns.com

Robert Hale is an imprint
of The Crowood Press

CHAPTER 1

The day started as had every other for the last twelve-month or so, with Melanie Hogan and her husband Caleb rising before first light to carry out various agricultural activities that had so far showed little or no return, notwithstanding the most strenuous exertions and unremitting efforts on the part of both husband and wife. This morning, their work entailed planting seed, which, if the experience of the last year taught them anything at all, was not likely ever to grow to maturity. As they sipped their coffee, the sky outside their little home still almost black, Caleb said, 'I do not know what is to become of us if there is not soon some rain. That seed we planted three weeks ago shows no sign of sprouting.'

'Don't take on so,' replied his wife. 'It is not in reason that this dry spell should go on much longer. Not at this time of year.' Although she spoke these cheery and comforting words in a bright sort of voice, she was desperately worried. Even by going on short commons herself, there was barely enough food to satisfy the children's hunger. She conceived it as her duty though to reassure her husband and lend him her support in any way possible; even if it meant half starving herself to make what little rations they did have go a little further.

By 1876, when Caleb Hogan took the decision to uproot his family and claim the hundred and sixty acres to which he was entitled under the Homesteader's Act, most of the more fertile and hospitable parts of the Great Plains had already been settled. So it was that his section was in a bleak and windswept corner of Nebraska, almost in the foothills of the Rocky Mountains. Thirty acres of the hundred and sixty were taken up not by arable land, but by a huge, craggy outcrop of bare rock that loomed above their fields and cast a long shadow over their home in the late afternoon and evening.

The children were not yet awake, so Melanie and her husband talked in hushed voices for fear of disturbing them. Zachariah, who was coming up to fifteen years of age, was almost as much use about the place as a grown man. His sister Elizabeth though was just eleven and still very much a child. It was when she considered the hardships that her children had faced and were like to face for the foreseeable future, that Melanie's heart became leaden and she half-wished that they had never left the cramped, two-room apartment in Independence. Still and all, there it was. For good or ill, they were here now and needs must make the best of things.

After she and Caleb had spent the better part of two hours labouring in the pre-dawn of what promised to be a glorious April morning, they returned to the cabin and Melanie prepared a meagre enough breakfast for the whole family. They had a little milk and some oats, and these she boiled up together and brewed another pot of coffee. It was after rousing the children that she glanced out the window and saw that they had company. It was barely seven, which was, thought Melanie, a strange time for anybody to come visiting. She said to her husband, 'Caleb, there's three men without as I think wish to speak with us.'

Although he had no particular apprehension of danger, Caleb Hogan stood up and went over to where his fowling piece, an ancient scattergun, hung on the wall. He reached it down, cocked both hammers and then walked out to see what the strangers might be wanting.

The three riders sat at their ease. Although they evidently wished to speak to the occupants of the little soddy, none of them seemed inclined to dismount and knock on the door, preferring simply to wait until the person within the little dwelling came out to wait upon them. Two of the men looked like young cowboys or ranch-hands, being clad in simple, work-clothes. The third presented a very different aspect, being a man in his riper years, perhaps forty-five or fifty years of age. His dress would have been better suited for a railroad journey than going on horseback through farmland, wearing, as he was, a fine suit of dark blue broadcloth. This individual had a pleasant, good-natured and open countenance and when he saw Caleb Hogan emerging from his home, he greeted him cheerily, crying, 'A very good morning to you, neighbour. I hope it ain't too early for to be paying calls?'

'I been up these two hours,' replied Hogan, 'It's not so early as all that.'

This seemed to amuse the man, because he chuckled and said, 'Well, I reckon that's set me right! "Go to the ant thou sluggard", as it says in the Good Book. That would about fit the case here, hey? I'll allow you got the drop on me there, you farmers put the rest of us to shame with your early rising.'

Caleb Hogan said nothing, but merely stood waiting to see what would next be said. He had had this fellow pointed out to him in town and knew him to be an important landowner, whose property lay away to the north of Hogan's own land. There were rumours that Andrew McDonald, for that was the fellow's name, was irked by the proliferation of little farms that were springing up around him now and having the effect of hemming in and environing his pastures. At length, Hogan said, 'It's right nice to see you, Mr McDonald, but the day is wearing on and I've a heap o' chores to attend. So if you could let me know to what I owe the pleasure of seeing you here today?'

'Ah, a man after my own heart. You won't waste words. I'll come straight to the point. I've herds to pasture and I want all the land I can get for them. All these little bits of land that Washington parcels out and gives to you fellows is making my life devilish difficult. Devilish difficult.'

Elsewhere on the plains, not just in Nebraska but also in Wyoming and other territories, there had been bitter 'range wars', in which men who had grown wealthy from allowing their cattle to roam wild across the open range became angered by the number of settlers who built fences and blocked off the range. Caleb Hogan had not heard of anything of the sort happening in this part of the country though and wondered uneasily of this was the prelude to a threat. It swiftly proved to be nothing of the kind though, as McDonald at once made plain. He said, 'I've a mind to buy up some of the land which has been farmed hereabouts by honest men like yourself. I'll pay good cash money for it. Fact is, I'm here to offer you five hundred dollars this very minute, if you'll sign over your acres to me. I'd say that's a right generous offer.'

Melanie had come to the door by this time and was standing and listening to what was being said. She knew that it wasn't her place to interrupt, but could not help but wonder what was going on. Her mind worked rapidly, as she mentally listed all those whose claims actually bordered Andrew McDonald's land and wondered if they too had been offered five hundred dollars to leave their land. Why, there must be four other settlers living just between here and the edge of McDonald's spread. Was he handing out thousands of dollars, willy-nilly, to get the sparse and unproductive grassland that comprised the plots of land granted to former soldiers in this area? It didn't sound likely to her.

Caleb's mind had perhaps been working towards the same end, for he said slowly, 'You fixin' for to purchase every section hereabouts? That'll cost you a pretty penny and no mistake.'

MacDonald's smile did not falter. He said, 'I lay my plans deep. Don't you set mind to what land I might be acquiring, but just look to your own interest. I've five hundred dollars for you this minute, were you only to sign a document that my attorney'll draw up.'

Rubbing his chin meditatively, Caleb said, 'Well, I thank you kindly for the offer, but I'm my own master here. I don't reckon as I'm wanting to go back to working for another. So the answer will have to be no.'

'No percentage in being hasty,' replied McDonald, with undiminished amiability. 'I'll come by tomorrow and see if we can't reason that case out to our mutual advantage. Good day to you now.' With that, he and the other two riders set off north at a gentle trot, as though they had all the time in the world and this little visit had been a matter of small importance to them.

Turning and seeing his wife standing at the door of their home, Hogan said, 'What do you make to that?'

'Something don't listen right about it, is what I think.'

'I's thinkin' the self-same thing, my own self,' said Hogan. 'Something here ain't right. Sides which, I haven't even proved up on this place. I've no legal title to it for another year yet. And why offer me all that money? I've a notion that when he comes back tomorrow, he has it in mind to raise the ante and see how much I'll settle for.'

'What say one of us ride over and see if he's made similar offers to others? This place'd be no manner of use to him without others also give up their land. He couldn't even get his cattle here without trespassing on others' land; leastways, not as things stand now.'

Under the 1862 Homestead Act, any man who had not taken up arms against the United States government during the War Between the States was entitled to claim a hundred and sixty acres of land in the west. All that was required was that he and any dependants lived on the land for five years and improved it by cultivation. Then, he could file title to it and it belonged to him and his descendants in perpetuity. Caleb Hogan knew all this well enough and was accordingly puzzled about the offer of money for surrendering the land on which he and his family were now living. Why, it wasn't even his and would not be for another four years! Even to sell it would be, from all that he could see, an illegal act.

Later that day, while his wife tended to domestic affairs, Hogan rode over to see what, if anything, his neighbours could tell him. It didn't take long to discover that not one of them had been made any offer of the sort that he had received that morning; which immediately aroused his suspicions that there was something irregular about the whole business.

When first the family arrived in Nebraska a year earlier, travelling in an open wagon hauled by a pair of oxen, they found nothing but a hundred and thirty acres of flat, scrubby grassland, with the rocky bluff towering above it. A fresh water stream flowed from the bluff and meandered through their land, which was a mercy, for it meant that whatever else they lacked, there was no shortage of potable water. Like everybody else, the Hogans constructed a small hut by cutting up rectangular blocks of turf to use as bricks. Because these were cut from the sod, such dwellings became known colloquially as 'soddies'. For the next year, life was one long and unremitting grind of hard work and severely restricted rations. To begin with it had all seemed worthwhile, because Caleb Hogan was no longer beholden to any employer for his daily bread. Lately though, both he and his wife were beginning to wonder if the game was worth the hardships that were part and parcel of being a pioneer in those parts. A drought had gripped the plains for much of the winter and planted seed showed no present sign of germinating; despite it being springtime.

After her husband had ridden off to see what might be happening elsewhere in the district, as regarded any other generous offers being made for uncultivated land, Melanie Hogan attempted, not for the first time, to teach her daughter the correct way of kneading dough and turning it into something resembling a loaf of bread. As she set out the board and took out the sack of flour, she said to her son, 'Zac, I want you to take this here pail and fetch water from the stream. You're to spend an hour or so watering those seeds that your pa and I planted 'fore you and your sister had even stirred from your slumbers.'

'Lordy Ma, way the ground is now, it's dry as a bone. A drop o' water won't help none. It'll run straight off. We need a rainstorm or two to do any good.'

His mother looked at him and said, 'You think I don't know that? It'll be better than nothing though. Off you go, now.'

The boy seemed disposed to linger, and at the door he paused and said, 'What did those men want earlier?'

'I don't rightly know and that's the truth of the matter. Something's afoot and I don't know what. Your father's gone off to ask around. Off with you now.'

Two things emerged clearly from Caleb Hogan's visits with his neighbours. First off was where not one of them had been offered a single cent to vacate their land; he alone had been favoured with such an offer. This in itself was quite sufficient to cause Hogan to smell a rat and suspect that something queer was going on. The second point was that, like him, the other settlers were almost at breaking point and a number were considering abandoning their claims and returning to civilization. If he was any judge of such things, Hogan guessed that unless there was a dramatic turnabout in fortunes, then within a year at most, this part of the plains would be all but deserted again. Which made Andrew McDonald's offer of such a large sum of money all the more puzzling. A little before midday, Hogan turned the mare around and headed back home to eat.

After he had apprised his wife of what had passed between him and those who lived nigh to them, the afternoon was spent in the usual round of activity. The children collected stones from the ground, which had lately been broken for the first time since

14

Creation by having a plough dragged across it. Hogan himself led the oxen in this endeavour while his wife busied herself in trying to put together some kind of meal for them, when the day's work was completed. They had hardly any lamp-oil left and so the whole family had taken to retiring at nightfall, as soon as there was no longer enough light to work by.

The previous day, Hogan had brought down a small buck and this meant that the meal that evening was an uncommonly fine one, with as much meat to eat as any of the family could desire. True, there were no side vegetables, but with some of the bread that had been baked that day they were all able to fill their bellies. While they ate, Hogan remarked, 'Something's not right about that affair this morning. It troubles me.'

'Like as not, it don't signify overmuch,' replied his wife reassuringly, although she too was uneasy about the business. 'They do say as some folk has more money than sense.'

'Happen so, but there's a mystery there. I don't like it.'

After they had all eaten their fill and the wares were washed up and stacked away, Hogan led his family in prayer. He was a devout man and one of the reasons that he had wished to leave Independence and come out here into the wilderness was that he viewed some of the goings on in the city as being on a par with what had been seen in the olden days in

Sodom and Gomorrah. He knew how that had ended and wished to lead his folks to safety from the wrath that he thought might be about to descend from the Lord.

'Oh Lord,' said Caleb Hogan, 'We thank you for all your mercies, specially giving us full bellies this day. Protect us from evil and help us all to grow in righteousness day by day. We ask all this in the name of your son, who came to save us.' After this short act of thanksgiving, he and his wife and children retired for the night.

Three hours after they had all laid themselves down to sleep, Melanie was awoken by the flickering glare of flames outside. She did not at first understand what this might portend, but before she could rise and go to the window to see what was going on, there came a fusillade of shots, one of which penetrated the turf wall, sending a shower of powdery earth over her.

The shots woke Caleb, who sprang to his feet and snatched down his scattergun. Melanie cried out in alarm, 'Caleb, don't rush out there. It could be anybody.'

The children had also been woken by the gunfire and were sitting up, bewildered and scared. Instructing them to stay where they were and not to stand up, Melanie hurried after her husband, who had marched angrily out through the door to confront whoever was firing near his home. She reached the door a second or two after Caleb and stood on the threshold for a moment, unable fully to understand the scene before her.

There were a half-dozen riders gathered outside and some of them were carrying flaring torches that gave off a pleasant aroma. She guessed that these were pine knots that they had kindled before announcing their presence by loosing off their weapons. A disconcerting circumstance was that each man's face was concealed by an old sugar sack, in which large, ragged holes had been cut so that they might see out. When she had been a little girl, such things had been known as 'spook masks'. It was plain as a pikestaff that these men were up to no good, but what business they might have with she and her husband was more than Melanie Hogan was able to fathom.

Caleb stood in the flickering torchlight, looking round at the men, trying to figure out the play. He held the shotgun ready in his arms, not pointing at anybody in particular, but clearly ready to bring it up to aim should the need arise. He said loudly and with no trace of fear in his voice, 'One o' you boys care to tell me what's a goin' on?' There was no answer.

There was something eerie about those six riders, just sitting there without speaking. Even the masks, the kind of thing that children make to play with, seemed somehow sinister. Hogan spoke again, saying, 'Well, if'n you're none of you going to oblige me with an explanation, then maybe you'd all care to get off my land?'

Just when it appeared to Melanie that the whole thing was just a piece of nonsense and something they might all laugh about in the morning, one of the riders raised a carbine that he had evidently been holding loosely and out of sight and fired a single shot at the ground. By ill chance, the ball struck a rock on the ground and ricocheted upwards, taking Caleb Hogan in the chest. For a moment or two, he struggled to remain upright and it looked as though he was minded to fire back with the shotgun, but it was all that he could do to stay on his feet. After wavering for a few seconds, the weapon fell from his nerveless fingers and he collapsed to the ground. At that moment, one of the riders shouted a word of command and the whole troop of them wheeled round and cantered off into the night, flinging their burning brands away as they rode off.

Melanie rushed to her husband and knelt down at his side. There was a new moon, which meant that the only illumination came from the sparse gleam of starlight. She called back over her shoulder to her son, who was now standing in the doorway, fearful perhaps of coming all the way out into the open, 'Light the lamp and fetch it. Hurry now!'

Caleb was breathing heavily, and she could hear a rasping, gurgling sound each time he drew in air. A cold hand seemed to clutch at her heart, for she had

18

worked in a hospital during the war and the noise that she now heard did not, to her ears, presage good news. 'I didn't think as they'd shoot me,' said her husband in a surprised tone, 'I thought they was only hoping to scare us.'

'Hush now, don't tire yourself by talking. Where's that boy got to with that blamed lamp?' At this moment Zachariah emerged with the lamp, which shed its soft glow over the little tableau of husband and wife. Melanie said, 'Fetch it closer, son. I want to see what's what.' Now that she had a clearer view of the wound that her husband had taken, she was anything but comforted. Just as she had suspicioned from the bubbling sound when he sucked in his breath, the wound was in his chest, a little to the right of centre. She was no physician, but guessed at once that it had struck the lung on that side. Trying to keep up Caleb's spirits, she said lightly, 'Ah tush, it's no more'n a scratch. I'll warrant you took worse than that in the war and scarcely broke step.'

Her husband was not deceived. He smiled crookedly and said, 'You allus was a terrible liar! I know what mischief is wrought. Even had we a doctor near at hand, this'd do for me.'

'Don't say so,' said Melanie despairingly, 'I say it will be fine.'

The two children had both come out now and were looking down on their father, where he lay dying. He said with a faltering voice, 'The two o' you bend down.

I'd give you my blessing.' The boy and girl knelt down; both had tears in their eyes, for they had sensed that this was the end for their pa. Caleb smiled at them and said, 'Zac, you look after your ma. And you, Betty, do as you're bid by your mother, you hear me now?' Both of them nodded dumbly, their hearts too filled with sorrow to speak. Then, as peacefully as if he was laying in his bed and drifting off to sleep, Caleb Hogan closed his eyes, took one long, shuddering breath, let it out slowly and did not again draw breath.

The three figures kneeling beside the corpse did not move for a full minute. Even Melanie, usually so practical and resourceful, had not the least notion how to proceed further. It slowly dawned upon her that she was now utterly alone and wholly responsible for her children's welfare and lives. She felt as though the weight of this was crushing her down. Always, Caleb had been there to aid and support her; taking the chief of any burden upon his own broad shoulders. She said, 'There's no point in any of us trying to sleep more this night. You two go into the house now and I'll make provision for your pa.'

Even as she spoke, Melanie was working out that she would need to report this affair to somebody in town. There was no regular law in Benton's Crossing, the town was too small for that, but there was a Justice and also a minister. Maybe one of those would do. She would also have to arrange, she supposed, for a funeral. While she was thinking all this, Melanie

Hogan marvelled at her own calmness. It was as though she were outside this disaster and looking down upon those enduring it. If it were not so, then she would have run around, screaming like a madwoman. What she and her children would do next, she had no idea at all. She'd no living kin, other than those who lived some miles to the east, along the Niobrara. It would hardly be possible to expect any help from them, considering their current circumstances. Well, that would all keep until after the funeral. Again, she was amazed that the word could come into her head and not drive her frantic with horror and fear. I guess that's what it's like, she thought calmly, when there are children to care for. Your own grief has to be set to one side, until a more convenient time.

It was a grim enough night and neither she nor her son or daughter ever forgot the horror of it. In later years, all three of them would use that night as a touchstone for any bad experience that they were undergoing. Whatever it was, when compared with those dreadful hours between the murder of Caleb Hogan and the rising of the sun the following day, any other trial paled into trifling insignificance.

At one point, Elizabeth said, 'What's Daddy doing now outside? Won't he be cold?' It struck her mother that the child did not really have any understanding of death; how should she, never having encountered it before?

21

Melanie said to the child, 'Your pa's gone to join those who have been promoted to glory, Betty. He's with the Lord now. You know how powerful strong he was for Jesus? Why, that's why he wanted to name the two of you Zachariah and Elizabeth.'

This promised to take the little girl's thoughts away from the death of her father, for she said, 'Remind me again, Ma. Who are we named after?'

'Why, John the Baptist's mother and father, of course. Zachariah and Elizabeth had given up on having any children, for she was growing old. But the Lord gave her a baby at about the same time that Mary was a-carrying of Jesus. Elizabeth and Mary were cousins, you know.'

Somehow, the night wore away until dawn and Melanie prepared breakfast for them all before harnessing up the oxen to the wagon and drawing her dead husband's body to town to make any necessary arrangements.

CHAPTER 2

Andrew McDonald came to the western end of the Great Plains towards the back-end of 1848. He had some seed-money, a few hundred dollars that he had acquired in the course of a long and protracted poker game. It was enough to buy him a few head of cattle, which he allowed to roam across the open grassland that stretched for hundreds of miles in every direction. Sleeping, to begin with, in a tent, McDonald built himself a log cabin, which he later extended until it became a grand farmhouse. The dozen cattle become first a score and then a hundred. The McDonald ranch flourished. When the great War Between the States began in 1861, a contract was secured to supply the Union Army with beef and very profitable it was too. It was when the war ended that things began to go wrong for Andrew McDonald.

The prosperity of ranchers such as McDonald was

founded upon the very existence of the open range. It cost literally nothing to feed and water the mightiest herd of cattle. There was unlimited, if scanty and innutritious, grass to be had and no shortage either of fresh water in the form of rivers and streams. The herds could be left to roam and only rounded up when there was need to sell, slaughter or transport them elsewhere. This meant that for much of the time there was hardly any expenditure to worry about.

Ranchers like McDonald had grown so used to this way of life that it came as a shock when the government in Washington began to allocate parcels of land for all who wanted them, on the very grasslands upon which the economy of the ranchers relied for their livelihood. The Homesteader's Act was passed in the second year of the war, but it wasn't until the war had ended that the full effects were felt. By then, a new invention was being freely used by the settlers – barbed wire. As the plains were carved up in this way and the cattle from the big ranches were no longer able to wander freely, seeking sustenance and water where they would, there were some who resorted to violence to maintain their old way of life. Fierce 'range wars' were fought between the ranchers and the newcomers, who were each determined to establish their own little farms.

Some men, Andrew McDonald was one of them, held aloof from all this until they could see which way the wind was blowing. The government was not minded to let citizens take the law into their own hands and use deadly force to settle disputes with their neighbours. It could clearly be seen where this sort of thing could end when looking at the events of 1861 to 1865 and the men in Washington were not going to allow matters to drift in that direction again. Federal troops were used to suppress the fighting that flared up sporadically from these disputes, and it struck McDonald that he would be a fool to try and drive away the homesteaders by using violence against them. However, he could ill-afford to let matters take their own course either.

During the good times, when money was flowing in freely to his ranch, McDonald had spent pretty freely as well; letting the money flow out more or less as it flowed in. Why not? What was the point of money if not to enjoy it and allow it to enhance one's way of living? There scarcely seemed any reason to save any of the money that was floating around; there would always be the opportunity to make more, should need arise. Like so many others, it was not until the disaster was upon him that McDonald saw that his entire way of life was over and finished, and that if something unexpected did not intervene to rescue him, he would be left little better than a pauper. Whenever money had not been readily available for whatever reason, McDonald had borrowed without hesitation. He had obtained a mortgage on his land and not even considered how it would be if this was to be called in at short notice. Well, with the problems facing ranchers like him, that was just the very time that the bank became nervous and demanded that he settle up with them. They required the balance of just over seven thousand dollars to be paid in full by the end of the month. He had twenty-five days to stave off penury and ruin.

As usual, it was his wife who showed Andrew McDonald the best path out of his predicament. For a quarter of a century, Josephine had been at his side, urging him on and pushing him to take any risks that she thought were worth the hazard. Now, faced with the loss of everything that they had worked for, Josephine had come up with the solution. If that solution entailed mayhem and murder, then so be it!

The homesteaders who had flooded this part of Nebraska in the years following the end of the war objected strenuously, and understandably, to having cattle driven over their newly ploughed fields. Nobody minded though people on foot crossing their land. That was only neighbourly; to let anybody who wished to take a short-cut through fields, so long as no harm was done to crops and so forth. Josephine McDonald was a great walker and the farmers thereabouts were used to the sight of her, walking briskly to and fro. She even walked the four miles to town when the mood was upon her. One of her favourite walks was up onto the bluff that towered above the Hogans' land. It was while making her way across the stream that sprang up on the bluff and ran down onto the plain below that Josephine found something that interested her greatly. This was the day before the murder of Caleb Hogan.

When she had returned from her walk up onto the bluff that day, Josephine said to her husband, 'Well, any good fortune with the bank?'

He shook his head. 'Nothing doing. We can't find several thousands of dollars in the next month, we're done for.'

'Not while I have breath in my body, we're not,' she replied and reached into her reticule, taking something from it. 'What do you make to this here?' she asked tossing something down – a small shower of material onto the desk at which McDonald was sitting. The objects, whatever they were, fell with heavy thuds. Andrew McDonald picked the items up. They were small and misshapen lumps of yellowish metal, the largest of which was about half the size of a bullet. He hefted this in his hand and then drew a fingernail across the surface, noting with interest the line that he was able to score in this way.

'Is this what it looks like?' asked McDonald, almost faint with relief at seeing a possible way out of the trap in which he found himself.

'If it looks to you like a nugget of alluvial gold, then I dare say that's what it is, yes,' replied his wife tartly, 'And I've a notion that there's a pretty fair supply of it, just for the picking. You know my pa made his money through prospecting. I recollect him telling me about the geology of gold-bearing rocks. Sometimes, there'll be a vein o' gold that runs deep under the ground and then suddenly emerges up into the air, where it can be seen.'

'Lord a mercy, Josephine,' cried McDonald, 'What are we waiting for? Let's go off and fetch it.'

'Just wait up. There's a little snag, but nothing we can't fix.'

'Well? What's to do?'

Briefly, Josephine McDonald apprised her husband of the state of play; that the gold was on the parcel of land belonging to the Hogans and that if anybody had a legal right to the minerals there, it was them and not the McDonalds. She said, 'Oft-times, native gold like that goes hand-in-hand with artesian streams like that up on the bluff. You know the gold rush across in the Black Hills? I'll wager that the bluff is part of the same formation, an outcrop as they say.' She ended by setting out a course of action that might just save their way of life.

'You reckon as I should offer him a right good price for the land, to start off with?' asked McDonald thoughtfully. 'But then if he don't accept, we should get a bit rough?'

'Time's pressing. That bank won't hold back. We ain't careful, we'll find our belongings being sold at public auction. You know that.'

Andrew McDonald thought over what his wife had said. As usual, she had put her finger right on the problem and, also as usual, she had seen a solution to the difficulties that faced them. He said, 'Well, I guess that you might have a point here. Unless. . . .'

'Unless what?' Josephine asked impatiently.

'Unless we could maybe collect the gold, pan the stream or what have you, without telling 'em.'

'That won't answer. To get the amount we're going to need to settle that mortgage, we're going to want a team of men, all you can spare, up on the bluff digging and hunting for gold. I reckon there's a vein of the stuff. Somewhere along the bank of that stream. These little bits have been worn away from it.'

'Enough to settle our difficulties?'

'We work hard and fast, yes I reckon so.'

So it was that the following day, Andrew McDonald rode on down to the Hogans' soddie and made what he considered to be a handsome offer to take over their land. After speaking to his wife, he had himself taken a walk up to the bluff and found more flakes and particles of gold in the stream bed, confirming what Josephine had told him. All this without so much as using a pan! The precious metal was purely waiting to be picked up out of that little rivulet. And, like his wife had said, there was surely a thick vein of gold somewhere nearby and when they found that then their problems would all be over. Why, maybe the bluff was just loaded with gold and he could give up herding cattle and just set up as the owner of a gold mine. Such thoughts were swirling through McDonald's brain as he fetched up at the Hogans and it was consequently a crushing disappointment to find that the man didn't leap up and bite off his hand for the five hundred dollars that was on offer.

There was something stubborn and mule-like about the visage of Caleb Hogan, which caused McDonald to think that the man was not going to allow himself to be buffaloed into any hasty decision about the disposition of his property. He was determined, by the look of things, to consider matters carefully and chew them over for a spell; the very last thing that Andrew McDonald desired to happen. For one thing, time was pressing, and for another, if this fellow thought too long and hard, then maybe he would ask himself if something else lay behind the generous offer that had been made to him. It wasn't to be borne! McDonald decided then and there that he would move rapidly to the next stage of the plan that his wife had suggested; that was to say frightening the man and forcing his agreement under a threat to him and those whom he held dear.

The half-dozen hands who had been commissioned to menace the homesteader had been paid a bonus only to scare the man, not commit murder. They had been instructed to dress up something like the Ku Klux and to fire a few wild shots about, just as an indication of how things might end if Hogan didn't see sense and take the easy path. One of those in the party though was a worthless, sodden wretch by the name of Dave Jackson. This young man was seldom sober after sundown and on this night had taken more drink than was good for him. It was Jackson who had fired the shot directly at the wall of the soddie, the one that had showered Melanie Hogan in dried earth after she had awoken that fearful night.

Something about Caleb Hogan's demeanour had put Jackson out of countenance when he walked out of his mud hut. For one thing, he was carrying a gun and did not look as though he would scruple to use it if need arose. For another, there was not the slightest trace of fear in the man's face and that irked Dave Jackson for some reason. Here they all were, seated on their mounts wearing masks and carrying flaming brands, and this sod-busting oaf just stood there eyeing them coldly, like he would be happy to set to with them should this be needful. So irritated was Jackson by this that he decided to give Hogan a scare, nothing more than that. Raising his rifle, Jackson fired towards a spot some five or six feet from the farmer's feet.

Some of the flatter stones that had been dug up from the earth when ploughing the land had been carried to the house and some attempt made at providing a dry area there, less muddy than the rest of the ground. By unlucky chance, the ball that Jackson fired ricocheted off one of these rocks and flew straight between two of Caleb Hogan's ribs, inflicting a mortal wound on the man's lung. It was all the merest ill fortune, which nobody had planned for or desired.

Scripture says that 'Morning brings counsel', which is perhaps merely another way of saying that what perplexes us greatly during the hours of darkness can sometimes seem much simpler when the sun rises. For Melanie Hogan, broken up by grief though she was, two things became apparent with the dawn. First off was where there was something exceedingly peculiar about this whole, tragic sequence of events. Why should a man offer five hundred dollars one minute and then organize a murder the next? It wasn't in reason. The second point that stood out with crystal clarity was that her husband's death must be avenged. One way or another, somebody would have to pay for having a hand in ending the life of Caleb Hogan. If the law would take on the job, then all well and good. If not, then she herself might be compelled to serve as the instrument of justice. Of one thing, she was quite certain; payment would have to be made for this terrible crime. In the meantime, she was more concerned about her children and how they were to be able to cope with the death of their father.

In the usual way of things, so far in Zachariah and Elizabeth's lives, death had come only to those who were aged or ill. Explaining the death of a grandfather to a child, or that of a person who has been stricken with the bloody flux or something similar, is not a pleasant duty, but can at least be represented as somehow being the natural order of things. The sudden and violent death of a parent though, is altogether different. It strikes at the very heart of a child's existence and comes like a bolt of lightning from a clear, blue sky.

The only remedy that Melanie Hogan could see for the case was to approach it all in a matter-of-fact and practical fashion. There had been tears and lamentations during the night, with her little daughter drowsing off fitfully and then awakening sobbing and heartbroken. Zachariah was more stoical, at least on the surface, but it was plain that he too was shaken to the core by what had happened. As the sun rose and shed its light through the window of their little home, Melanie said briskly, 'Now you two, we need to think on what's to be done this day.'

'What would you have me do, Ma?' asked her son, which made his mother's heart swell with pride. He was little more than a child, but had already decided that he had to play the part of a man now.

'Your father was killed unjustly,' Melanie said bluntly, feeling that rough words might discourage any renewed outbreak of sobbing from Betty, 'And I must go to town to make enquiries about the best way to proceed.'

'You mean the police?' asked Zachariah, who remembered how law and order had been kept back in Independence.

'It may be so. I don't rightly know. I believe that the nearest sheriff is some thirty miles from here. It will need to be looked into.'

'Are we going to stay here?' Betty enquired.

'I can't say, darling. Not until I've spoke with people in town. I won't leave you here though, you can both come along of me, if you will.'

In the ordinary way of things, the offer of a trip to town was sure to raise a smile from both the children, but the sombre nature of the projected expedition on this occasion was sufficient to leave them both looking serious and subdued about the idea. After preparing a little porridge for their breakfast, washed down with coffee, Melanie went out to the wagon and covered her husband's corpse with a tarpaulin. She could not allow the children to see such a dreadful sight as the dead body of their own father.

Andrew McDonald did not learn until that morning that one of his men had shot Caleb Hogan, and when he did find out he was furiously angry. One of the men who had consented to join the party sent to put fear into the owner of the bluff had come to him before breakfast that day and said that it was a terrible thing and that he was minded to lay an information against the perpetrator of the shooting.

'Don't be hasty now,' said McDonald soothingly, 'There's no percentage in rushing forward to such a course of action as that.'

'It ain't right,' said Seth Williams, who was that rare specimen – a devout and God-fearing cowboy. 'Shooting of a man for naught. You asked for us to go and give him a scare, which weren't precisely a sin, leastways not by my reckoning. But shooting a man, that's something else again. I want no part of it.'

It occurred to Andrew McDonald that this righteousness on the part of Williams might have a strong business end to it. It could be that the fellow was afeared of being caught up in a murder and wished publicly to exculpate himself in advance, should any charges be laid against him for being part of the gang. Aloud, McDonald said, 'Who fired the shot?'

'Who d'ye think? It was that drunkard Jackson of course. Don't it say in scripture, "Wine is a mocker and strong drink is raging"?'

'Happen so. Was Hogan hurt bad?'

'I couldn't say. He dropped like stone, so I'd guess so.'

McDonald thought matters over for a spell and then said, 'You've my word that I will deal with this. There'll be something extra in your wages too, to make up for the upset, you know.'

After getting rid of Seth Williams, McDonald went in search of his wife, who was bullying some of the men down by the barn. When he had drawn her aside for a private word and given her to understand what was what, she said, 'I'll get one of the boys to harness up the buggy and take me into town. If it's serious, then I should think that his wife is like to be raising Cain there. She ain't one to hold back when she's aggrieved, from all that I am able to collect.'

Benton's Crossing, towards which both Josephine McDonald and Melanie Hogan were bound that morning, was little more than a hamlet. It boasted a saloon, general store, church and four dozen houses. The total population did not exceed three hundred souls, including those of tender years. Those were the permanent inhabitants, but there were frequently half as many folk again who were just passing through. The little place was on a cattle trail and often men camped out with their herds on the edge of the town and came to buy provisions in Benton's Crossing or to get drunk, just as the mood took them. The one sign of civilization that the little town lacked was anybody to enforce law and order. There was a Notary Public, who was useful for drawing up the documents required for sales of livestock or land, but nobody competent to act over violations of criminal law. The notary actually held the post of Justice of the Peace, but in that capacity he was able only to try cases brought before him. He had no authority to investigate misdemeanours and felonies, still less to arrest anybody or bring them to justice.

The journey to town was not an easy one. Zac guessed that the bundle in back of the wagon was his deceased father, but little Betty was apparently oblivious. Melanie walked alongside, all the way to town, to save the ox from having to over-exert his self. Oxen were the slowest of God's beasts at the best of times and she didn't much fancy being stuck in Benton's Crossing with an exhausted ox that could go no further that day. When first they arrived to take up their claim, Melanie had gone with her husband to visit Thomas Canning, the notary, and she recalled where his office was. It was not really an office at all, but a neat little white-painted, clapboard house. Outside hung a shingle, which announced that Thomas Canning, Attorney at Law, carried out his business at this address. Inside the house, one room on the ground floor was given over to bookshelves, cabinets and boxes of papers.

'Report an unlawful killing, hey?' said Canning, when the nature of the business had been revealed to him, 'Well, that's a rare enough occurrence hereabouts, I will say.'

Melanie had left the children with the wagon, as she did not wish them to hear their father's death being discussed in this way. Canning continued, 'I'm sorry for your loss, Mrs Hogan, sorry for your loss.

What do you seek of me?'

'I want the murderer brought to justice.'

'Wait a moment, now. When you say murderer, you're jumping the gun a little. Could be murder, might be manslaughter, maybe an accident, even suicide. Impossible to say without an inquest.'

'You can conduct an inquest?'

'You need a sheriff to look into the case first.'

'The nearest being?'

'Fort Worth. Thirty miles as the crow flies.'

Melanie Hogan stared coldly at the fussy little man seated in front of her. She said, 'What do you suggest, I take my husband's body away over to Fort Worth?'

There was an uncomfortable moment, while Thomas Canning seemingly considered this proposal seriously. At last, he said, 'You want my advice, Mrs Hogan? You can't bring back your husband and you won't be able to stay on that land now, not without a man to work it. Were I you, I'd be inclined to return to the city or wherever it was you came from. Even if we can get the sheriff to come here, have you any evidence of who killed your husband? Witnesses? Anything other than your suspicions?'

The bereaved widow got to her feet and said quietly, 'All of which means that you don't want any trouble or upset and you'd rather I just vanished quietly. Well, you needn't think it for a moment.' Then she turned on her heel and left.

The angry departure of Melanie Hogan from the

notary's house was seen by Josephine McDonald, who had been lingering nearby for some little while, having suspected that if Hogan had been badly injured or, which God forbid, even killed, then the first thing would be somebody coming to town and trying to get the law in on the game. After the ox-cart had left, Mrs McDonald rapped smartly on Canning's door and, because her husband was a man of such consequence hereabouts, soon learned all she needed to know. She returned home immediately and spoke to her husband, and so started a chain of events that was to lead to not a few deaths over the course of the next sennight or so.

When he learned that the man whose land he had been so desirous of acquiring for his own benefit was dead, Andrew McDonald had at least the grace to feel a little ashamed. He had not sought the man's death, but it might certainly smooth the path a little to getting his hands on the gold that was up on the bluff. Because he felt guilty about the death, McDonald reacted by blaming somebody else for it. The perfect scapegoat was Dave Jackson; the man who had actually fired the fatal shot. No matter that Jackson had only been up at Hogan's place any way because of orders from McDonald himself. When the man came to see his boss, McDonald was brutally direct. He said, 'What do you mean by this? I asked you to go and put the fear of God into a man and you kill him. That won't answer for me, you know.'

39

Jackson looked at him in bewilderment and said, 'Well, there ain't a whole lot I can do about it now. Less'n you want me to try and bring him back to life again?'

'Don't bother with smart talk like that. You can take your things and clear out, you hear what I tell you?'

'You mean you're throwing me out? For an accident like that?'

'Accident be damned! A man's dead, you lumbering oaf. You've put your own neck at hazard and maybe mine too. Best thing you can do is get clear of this district and hope that nobody was fond enough of Hogan to want to avenge him. Here's your money up to yesterday.' He pushed across the desk a pile of silver dollars. In a daze, Jackson picked them up and left the room.

The agricultural recession that gripped the whole nation at that time was making it harder and harder for men like Dave Jackson to obtain work. When they could find a job, wages were being driven down by the glut of unskilled labourers who flooded the market. Jackson had been nicely off here, with accommodation provided and a good wage into the bargain. He had too a particular reason of his own for not wanting to leave the ranch right then, something connected with his reasons for turning up there in search of work in the first place. As he wandered over to the cabins to collect his few belongings, he was seized by a killing rage and decided that he would be revenged upon Andrew McDonald for casting him aside in this way, even though he had been following the instructions he had been given.

The trip to Benton's Crossing had been a fruitless one for Melanie Hogan, as she had suspected it would be before even setting out. The visit to the minister at the church was even less productive than going to the Justice of the Peace had been. She had not really thought it over, but assumed that because he was a Christian, the Reverend Edwards would simply provide a grave for her husband and read the service at his funeral. Caleb had, after all, attended church pretty regular. It turned out though that this was by no means sufficient to gain a place in Heaven, nor even in the little church's burying ground. The minister had asked what provision Caleb had made in life for the disposal of his body, when once he was dead. 'In short, did he belong to a burial club, insurance scheme or any such?' asked Reverend Edwards sympathetically.

'Nothing o' the sort,' said Melanie Hogan. 'We never had a cent to spare, but what it went on vittles for the little'uns. You know us settlers ain't exactly rolling in money, Reverend.'

'Quite so, quite so. The thing is, Mrs Hogan, that I'm not really running a charitable concern here.

There's bills to pay, all manner of expenses. That's the only reason I charge for burial plots and the holding of services for the dead and similar.'

'You mean,' said Melanie slowly, as the full import of the clergyman's words sank in, 'That if I don't shell out for a grave and your services to conduct the funeral, then my husband won't be buried in your ground.'

'I'm sorry. If I made an exception for one deserving case, then nobody would bother to save up at all and then without the various fees and so on, the church might fold up.'

She stared in disgust at this reptile, who had the effrontery to represent himself as a man of God, and said, 'I reckon as we can do the job by our own selves. You ever read that passage in the Book of Amos, the one as touches upon those who are hard-hearted towards the widow and orphan? You'll be judged by that text, mister, once you enter the afterlife.'

Despite the fact that her journey to town had yielded no good, Melanie Hogan nevertheless had felt it was a thing that had needed to be done. She should at least try and settle matters according to the law, it was what Caleb would have wanted. Caleb had been fond of quoting the Bible to illustrate the fruitlessness of an individual seeking to execute justice by his own self. 'Vengeance is mine, saith the Lord; I will repay', had been one of the verses that he used to bring out when anybody talked of getting their own back. Well, she had done her best to do the thing legally and there was nothing doing. If there was to be any vengeance for her husband, then she would have to undertake the job herself.

CHAPTER 3

In the old wooden chest that Melanie had brought with her from her home when she got married fifteen years earlier, at the age of sixteen, were various relics of her childhood. Caleb had not been at all keen on being reminded of his wife's antecedents and background and so she did not bring out the contents of the trunk when either he or the children were near at hand. Once in a while though, when she was alone or everybody was sleeping, she opened the lid and held various items in her hands and remembered the past. Now, in the presence of her children, she lifted the lid and reached inside.

First out was a long, irregularly shaped rod, which was something over three feet in length and only fitted in the chest by being carefully positioned at a diagonal from one lower corner of the box, up towards the lid. Her bow! She had such happy memories of learning to use it when she was a little younger than Elizabeth was now. 'What is it, Ma?' asked Zac. She passed the length of buffalo horn, with strips of sinew attached to it, to her son.

'What do you think it is?'

The boy took it in his hands and examined it carefully, turning it round so that he could look at it from all different angles. Then his face lit up and he said, 'Hey, it's a bow, ain't it?'

'It's my bow,' said his mother. 'Time was when I was never apart from that bow, not for, why it must have been two years, I guess.'

Betty's sweet little face wore a perplexed expression. She said, 'What were you doing with a bow, Ma? You're not an Indian.'

'Well, not exactly, chicken. But there's something you two need to know about your mother. Your pa, he didn't like to hear it talked of, but I always planned for to tell you about it some day, when you were both older, maybe.'

'Tell us about what?' asked Zachariah.

'Why, about your family. Meaning my family.'

The grief of losing their father was still raw on the children; it had only happened a little over twelve hours since and it struck Melanie that telling them a story about her own life and that of her mother and grandma might be a sovereign remedy for taking their minds away from the subject, at least for a few minutes. Her own sorrow she had put off quite deliberately until a later date. There would be time enough to grieve when she had settled scores with the men who had done this terrible deed. She said, 'Here's the way of it. . . .'

The famous Oregon trail, the route along which many wagon trains made their way west throughout the nineteenth century, began in a small way in the years before 1820. These were the days when the Oregon territory was being shared with the British and a few hardy souls settled in and around Fort Vancouver. At that time, almost the whole of the Great Plains was unexplored territory and those who chose to travel from the relatively civilized east to the Pacific coast took their lives in their hands. In the autumn of 1818 two families set off in three wagons from St Louis, on the Mississippi, and headed north-west. Jacob James and his wife Mary, along with his three children, comprised one of the families. The children were ten-year-old Martha, Samuel, who was six, and a babe-in-arms called Daniel. The other family consisted only of a married couple called Tom and Anne Clayton. Somewhere near the Niobrara river, a bunch of Indians ambushed the wagons and that, as far as anybody knew, was the end of the two families.

Almost twenty years later, in 1836, the army was trying to make the route to Oregon a little less hazardous for the pioneers who were now being actively encouraged to open up the land in the west. The Indians, chiefly Lakota and other more obscure branches of the Sioux nation, were being a mite troublesome and so an expedition was launched to pacify some of the Sioux, who were sometimes known as the Eastern Dakota or Santee. In the course of the fighting, a village in what would later be South Dakota was raided and, to the astonishment of the soldiers, two white women were found to be living there. To be more exact, there was one woman who was about thirty years of age and her daughter, who looked to be perhaps twelve or thirteen.

The grown woman, who had not spoken English since she was a child, turned out to be Martha James, who had been snatched by the raiding party back in 1818; when she was just ten. Four years later, she had been married to Wabasha, the chief of the Santee, and had borne him three children, two of whom were still living. Her boy was learning to be a warrior, but her thirteen-year-old daughter was in the village when it was captured by the soldiers. This child spoke English haltingly and in addition to her Indian name had been given by her mother the name 'Alice'.

It was unthinkable to the troops who had found the two white women that they could be left in conditions of such degradation and squalor, and so, very much against their own wishes, they were carried off back to civilization. It was found that some members of the James family still lived near St Louis and so the mother and daughter were reunited with their kin in an uneasy celebration that was widely reported in newspapers in Washington and New York. Neither Martha nor young Alice really settled down to life among white folk. It was easier for Martha, because, of course, until she was ten she had lived an ordinary and unremarkable life in St Louis. Her daughter though had been born and raised among the Santee Sioux and theirs was the only life she had known.

There were some awkward times, for instance when Alice ran away from her family and made it almost back to the territory of the Santee, but with time she settled down to a relatively normal life and even married when she had grown a little more used to the ways of white people. This did not really work out though and after the birth of her only child in 1847, a daughter whom she named Melanie, the marriage was ended by mutual consent.

In the meantime, Martha James' other child, Alice's brother, had inherited the chieftainship of the Santee Sioux, following the death of his father. This young man, whom his mother had secretly named 'Samuel' after her own brother, but who was known to the Santee as Cutting Knife, had no intention of returning to his mother's people. Being chief of one of the fiercest and most warlike tribes in the plains was far too attractive a way of life for him to wish to surrender it to live in a cramped house in a dirty city. When he heard that his sister and her child were not finding life easy, after the end of her marriage, he sent word that she could come back and live with the tribe once more. So began a recurring theme of Melanie Trent's childhood, visiting for periods ranging from a couple of weeks to a couple of years, the Indian side of her family.

Because Melanie's mother was fluent in the dialect spoken by the Santee Sioux and was moreover well-known to most of the tribe, having been born and raised among them, she was happier staying with them than she was living in town. Melanie made friends, picked up the language and soon enjoyed staying with the Indians almost as much as her mother did. Sometimes she and her mother stayed for a space, perhaps for a month or two in the summer. When Melanie was nine, they moved into a tepee and remained with the tribe until her eleventh birthday. On their return to St Louis, her family there put their foot down. The child found herself being sent to a strict, Catholic school away over in the east and for the next few years the nuns endeavoured to turn her into a properly brought up young lady. At fifteen, she fell violently in love with a young man who lived near the school. At sixteen, she eloped with Caleb Hogan and within the year was pregnant with her first child.

For all that he loved and adored his new bride, Caleb Hogan was well aware that there was something a little elfin and fey about her. The remedy, as he saw it, was that Melanie should forget all about her times living in the wild with the Indians. A life of regular domesticity and motherhood would, he supposed, drive all that sort of thing from her mind. So it was that for the next fifteen years, until the day that Caleb was killed in fact, the only time that Melanie ever thought about her strange childhood was when her family were all sleeping and she had a few moments to herself. It was at such times that she was wont to open up her chest and handle lovingly the relics that were hidden within it.

'And that's how it was,' said Melanie to her son and daughter, 'I just didn't set mind to those days much at all. 'Sides which, the raising of the two of you has taken most all my attention.' She smiled, to indicate that she was only joshing and that bringing up the children had been a joy to her, rather than a wearisome task.

'Doesn't that make you a ... a...?' asked Zachariah, in an embarrassed tone of voice.

'A what?' said Melanie briskly, 'A half-breed, you mean?'

Her son blushed crimson and began stuttering an apology. His mother said, 'Well my own ma was half Indian, so I reckon that makes me a quarter Indian.'

'Then me and Betty are ... what's a half of a quarter, ma?'

'You never was one for ciphering! A half of a quarter is an eighth, so you and your sister are both an eighth Sioux.'

'Holy Moses,' said Zac, staggered at this sudden and wholly unlooked for revelation, 'You mean I'm partly one of them who killed Custer last year at the battle of Little Big Horn?'

'That's a fact,' said Melanie. 'Maybe you see now why your pa was so all-fired keen on your not knowing about all that. I think he thought it'd confuse you or make you unsure where you belonged in the scheme of things. He saw how it was with me and my ma, you see. Sometimes one thing, sometimes the other. Never really fitting in anywhere.'

Elizabeth had said nothing so far, just sat there staring in amazement at her mother. She reached out her hand and touched her mother's face, saying, 'Is that why you tan so ready, Ma? You never burn or go red in the sun.'

'That's right, little one. See, there's some advantage to having Indian blood in your veins.'

Zachariah's face was troubled and he said, 'Why are you getting these things out now, Ma? What's to do?'

His mother looked at him steadily and said, 'It seems like nobody is minded to look into your father's death, son. It's not right that a man may be murdered and nothing done about it. If nobody else'll undertake the job, then I reckon I'll have to do it myself. I mean to find out what happened and set whoever did this wicked thing to judgement.'

Josephine McDonald said to her husband, 'Let me ride out and talk to Hogan's wife, woman to woman.'

'You mean tell her that one of my boys shot her husband? No, don't think it for a moment. What are you about, you aim to put a rope around my neck? You never hear of a conspiracy to murder? That's a capital felony.'

'No, you booby, nothing of the kind. I mean to tell her that I sympathize for the loss of her husband and that because she won't be able to stay on that land now, anyhow, we won't take advantage of the fact, like some folks would. We'll increase our offer, out of respect for her loss.'

'Increase our offer? Have you taken leave of your senses? We got her on the run. I didn't want any blood to be shed, but now it has been, then it works to our advantage. That woman'll be running fast as she's able.'

It was at times like this that Josephine McDonald wondered how it was that men ran this world of ours, rather than women. She said, 'If that woman suspicions for a moment that we killed her husband a-purpose, then she might dig in her heels and stay put out of spite. If I can convince her that the whole thing was a stupid coincidence and that we mean her and her kind well, then she's apt to cut and run. Offering another couple of hundred dollars will show how kind we are.'

'You know that this'll take all the cash money we have? There'll be nothing left to pay wages or aught.'

'We don't get hold of the gold up on that bluff right fast, then we won't have a cent to bless ourselves with. We got a matter of weeks to set this right. We need to get to work, acquiring that gold this very week.'

While the McDonalds were disputing about the advisability of increasing their offer to the widow Hogan, Dave Jackson was skulking about in a copse of pine trees up on the hillside that overlooked the McDonalds' ranch. He was mightily vexed at the way matters had turned out and determined to wreak some vengeance upon his former employer. To Jackson's way of seeing things, he had done Andrew McDonald the biggest favour by shooting that stubborn son of a bitch whose land McDonald was after for some unknown reason.

Jackson didn't yet know that he had killed a man stone dead the previous night and, it has to be said, he would not have been a mite bothered even if he had known. He had killed men before that night and would most likely do so again. The fact was that Jackson had only signed on as a cowboy with the McDonalds six months before because he wished to lay low for a spell. He was from time to time a road agent and robber and had, in the course of a robbery, happened to murder a whole, entire family in a town less than a hundred miles from Benton's Crossing. The details of how this chanced to occur are not important, but there had been so much anger and fury about the killings that Jackson knew that he had come within a whisker of being hunted down and hanged out of hand. So bloody had the crime been that it had even found its way into the newspapers and, fearing for his life, he had ridden hard and found work here.

There were two reasons for Dave Jackson to be hanging round the place where he had, until a few hours earlier, been working. The first was that he wished to do some harm to Andrew McDonald and get his own back on the man for being thrown out. Then again, Jackson was all but destitute and the pitifully small amount of money he had been paid off with would not keep him going for more than a week at most. In common with the other men working on the ranch, Jackson had no inkling of the terrible financial difficulties that were now threatening to engulf his boss. From all that he was able to apprehend, Andrew McDonald was as rich as Croesus and was sure to have money or goods about his home that would be worth stealing. What Dave Jackson was in desperate need of was a road stake, enough capital to tide him over while he was on the road and seeking a new way of making a living.

From his position behind the fir trees, the embittered man kept a watch upon the McDonald ranch and bided his time. Thought they'd seen the back of him, did they? Well, that just went to show how purely wrong they were. Those folks didn't know Dave Jackson and had no idea what he was capable of!

'I know that it's been a terrible business,' said Melanie to her children, 'but there's nothing for it but to grit our teeth and carry on. I'm as broke up with grief as can be, myself, but we can't sit down and give up. That's not the way at all.'

'What would you have me do, Ma?' asked Zac, who obviously felt that, as the man of the house now, he should do his best to stifle his feelings and take on any new responsibilities that his mother felt were suitable. 'Just tell me what's to do and I'll get on with it.'

His mother smiled approvingly and said, 'Well, it's a grim enough chore to begin with. It looks like the burying of your pa, God rest him, will have to take place here on our own land.'

'You want that I should dig a . . . hole?' The boy could not bring himself to utter the word 'grave'.

Before she could answer, they all three of them heard the sound of a rider approaching. Melanie picked up her husband's scattergun and, after telling the children to stay inside, went out to see who it might be. To her amazement, it was a woman, riding astride a magnificent piebald stallion. When this person caught sight of the shotgun, she reined in and said in a loud, but pleasant voice, 'There's no cause for concern. I mean you no harm.'

''What do you want here? I mind I seen you in town with the fellow who came by here, trying to buy this land from my husband.'

'Yes, my husband is Andrew McDonald. Look, we can't talk so. Do you mind if I get down and we can just talk face to face, like civilised beings?' Josephine McDonald swung her leg over the saddle as a prelude to dismounting. She stopped abruptly when there was a sharp click and Melanie Hogan raised the shotgun to her shoulders and drew down on the other woman.

'You set foot on my land and before God, I'll shoot you down,' said Melanie. 'Don't think for a moment that I'm bluffing you.'

Not wishing to put the question to the test, Josephine McDonald very slowly put her leg back over the saddle and fitted it into the stirrup. She might be as tough as all-get-out-and-push when bossing workers about on the ranch, but this was something else again. She hadn't any doubt that this hard-faced woman meant just precisely what she said. This view was confirmed when Melanie said, 'Don't speak a single word, you hear what I say now? Your husband tried to buy my land and when he refused to sell, my husband, the best of men who ever walked this earth, was gunned down. You think I'd write that off as a coincidence? I'll warrant you come here today to up your offer. Let me advise you, don't do it. Just turn your horse round and take yourself off. I already taken first pull on the trigger and it would be nothing to me to shoot you. It's plain you're in on this dirty game. Now git on out of here.'

And Josephine McDonald, who was viewed as a regular terror by all the hands on her husband's ranch and the equal of any man in shoe-leather when it came to pushing folk around and speaking roughly, simply did as she was bid and rode off without another word. The experience of staring down the barrel of a shotgun held by a grief-crazed woman who would like as not be happy to kill her had not been an agreeable one and Josephine could feel the cold sweat of fear trickling down from her armpits and running down her sides.

It was a novel and wholly unpleasant feeling to have the fear of God put into her by somebody, especially some no-count sodbuster's wife. By the time that she arrived home, Josephine was good and mad and went straight to her husband. As soon as she entered his study, he said, 'Well, did it work? She leaving?'

'No, she's as stubborn as they come. There's only one thing for it. I'll be bound she sets a store by those children of hers. That's the only thing that might work.'

Andrew looked at her in amazement and said sharply, 'What are you about? I'm not going to harm a child. You can't be serious.'

'Nobody's talking of harming anybody. I mean that we should take one of those children, the little girl for preference. Then give the mother a choice of signing away the property for a good sum of money and digging up from hereabouts or not seeing her daughter again.'

'I don't like the sound of it. I won't scare a child. We'll have to think of another way.'

'There is no other way. If we don't start collecting that gold within a week or two, there'll be no chance of getting enough to pay off that mortgage; never mind anything else. We'll be homeless, penniless beggars. This is our only hope.'

It took a lot of doing, but slowly Josephine talked her husband round to her point of view and in the end he allowed that taking one of the children and keeping them at the ranch for a day or two was the only possible way of changing Melanie Hogan's mind about the wisdom of selling her land to them. So it was that a weak but essentially decent man was persuaded to embark upon a course of action that, in his heart of hearts, he knew to be wicked. There were, of course, ranchers at that time who would have adopted an altogether simpler and more brutal way of solving the problem that they faced, by the simple expedient of hiring a gang of killers to wipe out the family who were blocking their path. The McDonalds though were not of this brand, and although they didn't shrink from trying to scare folk and, if necessary, cheat them out of their goods and land, they stopped short at plain murder.

Working together, Melanie Hogan and her son succeeded in excavating a grave about a hundred yards or so from their little home. It was nothing like the traditional six feet in depth, being barely half as deep. Digging through sun-baked and dry clay soil is no easy task though and digging even this shallow trench had left mother and son exhausted. Elizabeth sat watching as they worked, from time to time wiping a tear from her eye. Events were moving with breakneck speed; her father had been dead somewhat less that twenty-four hours and already they were interring him.

It was late afternoon when Melanie decided that there was little purpose in delaying further and that they might just as well carry out the melancholy task of burying her husband. She harnessed up the ox to the wagon and guided it nigh to the grave. The mortal remains of Caleb Hogan were wrapped in a tarp, which would have to serve for both shroud and coffin. With Zac's help, she somehow manoeuvred the corpse as gently as they could into the yawning hole in the ground. It was not a dignified proceeding, but there was nothing to be done about that.

It had been some little while since she had attended a funeral, but Melanie recalled the chief passages from scripture and, opening her husband's well-thumbed Bible, she read out as many of them as she was able to bring to mind; Job, Isaiah and Matthew. 'Man that is born of woman has but a little time to live . . . cometh forth like a flower and is cut down . . . in my father's house there are many mansions. . . .' The children were visibly affected, especially Betty, but that was only to be expected.

When they went back inside, Melanie announced that she would be going out for a spell and leaving the children alone. Elizabeth was dismayed to hear this and would have protested, but her brother said firmly, 'Hush up now, sis. If Ma says she has to go out, then she's good reason. I'll take care of you.'

'It's not in reason that I should go off alone at such a time without telling the two of you what I'm about,' said their mother. 'This is the way of it. Those rogues want this land so bad that they're prepared to do anything, even commit murder for it. They ain't after our neighbours' land, so it must be something we have, but those others living near at hand don't.'

'You any idea what it might be?' asked Zachariah, 'Something buried maybe. Like treasure?'

'I'd the same thought. But maybe it's more obvious than that. What have we on our claim that nobody else has?'

'Well, there's the bluff, but that couldn't be worth anything. Could it?'

'I don't rightly know, but I aim to go up there now and have a scout around. We never really set mind to that chunk o' rock. Just seen it as a blamed nuisance.'

While she talked to her son and daughter, Melanie changed her clothes. They all lived in what was essentially one room and so there was no shame about seeing each other unclothed. After she had removed her skirt and blouse, she picked out a pair of work pants that had belonged to Caleb and pulled those on, followed by one of his shirts. Then she did a strange thing.

Like all grown women, Melanie Hogan wore her hair coiled up on top of her head, only letting it down at bedtime. Now, she brushed out her tresses and, rather than tucking them up into a bun, she separated them into two parts, by brushing a parting in the middle of her head. Then she dextrously plaited first one side and then the other, leaving the braids hanging free almost to her waist. After she had fastened her plaits, she went to the chest in which she kept relics of her old life and pulled out a leather belt, to which was attached a large sheath, containing a dagger, by the size of it. This, she buckled around her waist. Turning to the children, she said, 'Well, how do I look?'

With her glossy black hair in plaits and the unfamiliar garb, along with the knife hanging at her hip,

Melanie Hogan did not look at all like their mother. It was Elizabeth who summed up what they were both thinking. She said, 'Why Ma, you look like an Indian!'

CHAPTER 4

Trail boss Chris Rigby had almost as much to lose as the McDonalds if the ranch went bust. He had been working for Andrew McDonald for six years and was more like a partner in the business than an employee. McDonald had told him how bad things had become and Rigby was now sweating blood at the prospect of having to start over again as a lowly cowboy, always assuming that he could even find a job as such, which was by no means certain with the current state of the American economy. It had been Rigby who led the group of men wearing spook masks to frighten the Hogans into giving up their land. That had failed though and now Chris Rigby was more or less resigned to leaving in a few weeks and making his own way again. It was not an enticing prospect. So it was that when McDonald approached him, on the afternoon that Caleb Hogan was buried, with a plan that could save them all, Rigby listened attentively.

The first thing Chris Rigby said, before his boss had got out more than a couple of sentences, was, 'I'll have no part in harming a child and that's flat.'

'Lord a mercy,' exclaimed Andrew McDonald, 'That what you think of me after all the years we known each other, Chris? Nobody's going to get hurt, least of all a child.'

'What's the scheme then?'

As Andrew McDonald explained it, the whole thing was no more than a bit of a lark, in which they entertained a child for a few days on the ranch and while the little girl was being cosseted and petted there, her mother would be prey to all many of unfounded fears and anxieties; the result of which would be that she would sign over the land to McDonald, while making a right good sum to set up her and her little ones elsewhere. It was a hare-brained enough plan and it is a sign of how desperate the two men were that they should even consider an idea so likely to lead to unforeseen diffi-culties. But there it was; by the time the sun had set that day, Chris Rigby, Andrew McDonald and his wife had positively engaged to snatch Elizabeth Hogan and effectively hold her to ransom.

Melanie was no sort of fool and it didn't take her all that long to figure out the play, once she had been up on the bluff and had a good look around. Having correctly identified the rocky, thirty acres as being at the heart of the matter, narrowed the field considerably. It wasn't hard to guess that there must be some mineral deposit there that the McDonalds wanted and that in turn really only meant one of two things: silver or gold. The sun was declining and casting its rays into various little corners of the landscape that were not in general illuminated, save at that time of day. It was this that provided an early resolution to the conundrum.

The only point of note on the rocky slopes of the bluff was the spring of fresh water that emerged from a crevice in one of the low cliff faces. This little torrent then bounded along a channel, which it had cut in the shale over the millennia, before running into the grassland that formed the chief part of the Hogans' land. It was as she approached the point where the water sprang from the ground that Melanie saw a glint of something flashing in the westering rays of the sun. For a moment she thought that her eyes had deceived her, but then, as she moved her head from side to side, she saw it again; a brilliant gleam, as though a spark of light lay on the bed of the stream.

Keeping her fixed upon the location where the flash of light had come from, Melanie walked slowly forward until she was at the bank of the little stream. There, among the pebbles and rocks, she could just see a faint gleam, which must have been what had reflected the sunlight. She paddled across the water, which was less than a foot in depth, and reached down, plucking up a tiny piece of shiny metal, no greater in size than a grain of rice. She could see at once what it was and immediately understood the whole of what had befallen her and her family over the course of the last twenty-four hours. Her mouth set in a grim line as she realized that all this misery had been caused by nothing more than gold fever. Well, she thought to herself, we'll just see if I can't bring home to those McDonalds the wickedness of what they have done and all for the sake of some cold metal. She turned back towards the house and strode angrily forward.

Every so often in life, some projected plan goes better than one could ever dream of and the whole enterprise flows so smoothly that one feels that success was preordained. That's how it was when Andrew and Josephine McDonald went out with Chris Bridges that night to try and get hold of Elizabeth Hogan, to use her as a bargaining chip in their negotiations with the child's mother.

The sanitary arrangements of the Hogan family were simple and crude. They had chamber pots for use at night and a latrine pit, dug away from the house, which was used during the hours of daylight. This was no more than a hole in the ground, shielded from view by a canvas screen, supported by a few stout posts. As it filled, a new pit would be dug and the old one covered over and abandoned. Elizabeth hated to make water in the presence of her family, even when they were sleeping, and so was in the habit of going out to the latrine at back of the house, even in the dead of night. So it was that at about two in the morning, about eight hours after Melanie Hogan had worked out what had brought about the death of her husband, a slight, white-clad figure could be seen in the moonlight, trudging from the Hogans' soddie towards the latrine pit.

The original plan had been for the three mis-guided and desperate fools to creep into the house in the dark and seize the little girl, if necessary tying up the mother and brother. They had brought the spook masks with them, to disguise their identities. As it was though, having left their mounts a fair way from the house, the three of them were actually gath-ered at the side of the building, when the door opened and Elizabeth Hogan trotted off in the direc-tion of the privy. They could scarcely believe their luck. It was like they'd gone hunting and the prey had consented to walk right up and offer itself to their guns.

Once the child was out of sight, concealed by the canvas screen, the three of them walked briskly towards their target. It would obviously be better if any species of commotion took place as far from the house as could be. Josephine McDonald in especial had a very clear and uncomfortable memory of the flinty-eyed woman who had drawn down on her with that scattergun. She had no wish to repeat the experience. If the present enterprise could be undertaken quietly, without bringing the child's mother into the action, that would suit Josephine right down to the ground.

Elizabeth was plainly surprised to find three adults waiting for her after she had answered her call of nature. There was no easy or pleasant way of accomplishing this part of the process and so Andrew McDonald settled for doing it as swiftly as he might. He went forward and swept up the child in his arms. She began to cry, but he clamped a hand over her mouth; not viciously, but with just sufficient force to suppress any noise. Then he went off at a loping run towards where the horses had been left. The other two followed him, his wife first stooping and leaving a little bundle where it must be seen by anybody making for the privy.

In a half-hour, they were all of them back at the ranch and Josephine had taken the frightened child to sleep in a room with her. They figured that not only would such a course of action be more fitting for a girl-child, it would serve to soothe and allay the child's fears. Josephine McAndrew said, 'You need not be afraid of us, Elizabeth. We want your mother to do something for us, something which will be to

68

her advantage. Yours too. Then, soon as it's done, why you can go home. You only have to spend the night here and we expect to hear from your ma by the morning. You'll see, it will be fine.'

The little girl said nothing, but stared at Josephine McAndrew with an inscrutable look on her face, which the other found disconcerting. She said, 'Well, what does that look mean, missy?'

For a second or two, she thought that Elizabeth was not minded to answer, but then she said quietly, but very distinctly, 'You wait 'til my ma comes for me. You'll wish you'd never been born.'

For a moment, Josephine thought that her ears had deceived her, but the expression on Elizabeth Hogan's face was as serious as could be. She was looking at the woman as though almost in pity, as at one who does not know the peril she is in. Josephine shivered, as though a goose had walked over her grave. Then she said briskly, 'There'll be no cause for any unpleasantness. Just hop into bed like a good girl and I'll sleep in this other bed, see? It'll be fine.'

In fact, the whole business could even at that point have passed off without any more bloodshed and harm, but it was not to be. They say that from little acorns mighty oak trees grow and the truth of this old adage was to be amply demonstrated in the coming weeks as Andrew McDonald's simple desire

for enough gold to pay off the mortgage on his property spiralled out of control and precipitated a series
of bloody battles, which formed a coda to the Sioux
uprising of the previous year.

By the privy, Josephine McDonald had deposited a
parcel containing the seven hundred and fifty
dollars, which was all that they could raise, along with
a land contract that needed only Melanie's signature
to make it legally binding. The effect of this would be
to transfer ownership of the whole hundred and sixty
acres to the McDonalds, in exchange for the sum of
seven hundred and fifty dollars. It was hardly necessary to spell out that the return of her child was also
contingent upon the signing of this document. From
all that the McDonalds could see, this was a generous
enough deal. Without a grown man to work the land,
there was no prospect of the homestead being developed and so Melanie Hogan and her children would
have to leave in any case. This way, they left with a
tidy sum of cash money as well. How could anybody
refuse such an offer? The logic was irrefutable and
yet when she rose the night following her daughter's
abduction, settling for having her child back in
return for vacating the land was not at all the first
idea that sprang to Melanie Hogan's mind.

It was Zachariah who first realized that Betty was
missing. He was up at about dawn and went out back
to make water. The little bundle lying near the
latrine pit puzzled him greatly and he could not help

but open it, discovering what looked to him to be a king's ransom in bills. He knew at once that something was amiss and ran back to the house to wake his mother. It was then that they found that young Elizabeth was not in her bed. His mother said, 'Run to the privy and check that she's not fainted there or something.'

'She not there, Ma,' said Zac, when he returned, 'There's not a sign of her to be seen. What shall we do?'

While her son had run to check if his sister was out back, maybe having fallen asleep or passed out, Melanie had unfolded the sheet of paper that was attached to the parcel of bills. As soon as she read it, everything became clear to her. It was at this point that, according to the McDonalds' reckoning, she would throw in her hand and do as they wanted her to. They had left two things out of their calculations though. In the first instant, having seen her husband gunned down in front of her not forty-eight hours earlier, Melanie Hogan was convinced that she had to do with an utterly ruthless bunch of killers who would murder her child at the drop of a hat. She could not be expected to know that Caleb's murder was purely accidental and that neither of the McDonalds would dream of harming anybody, let alone an innocent child. She believed, with some reason, that her daughter was in the hands of a gang of men who would stick at nothing.

71

The second factor that the McDonalds had not accounted for was that Melanie was partly Indian and had spent long enough among the Sioux during her formative years to learn that you never gave way to a threat, because that always ended badly. No matter how hard or protracted the struggle, if somebody tried to force you to do something under a threat, why you fought back any way you knew how.

So it was that when once she had weighed and measured all that she could figure out about the disappearance of her daughter, Melanie decided that there was nothing for it but to fight and fight hard. Any other course of action might lead folk to regard her as weak, and in that case they might actually harm Elizabeth. Even signing that wretched document might not be enough. She might sign it and then they would do away with her child anyway, maybe just to dispose of the evidence of what they had done and to avoid leaving a witness alive.

'We need to have a good breakfast,' said Melanie to her son. 'You're going on a little errand for me.'

'An errand? What you mean – riding into town? What about Betty?'

'This is for Betty. We need help to deal with this.'

'You mean the law?'

'No, I mean my kin. There's a heap of 'em live about fifteen, maybe twenty miles from here.'

Zac stared at his mother in surprise. 'You got folks living that close? How come we never seen them?'

'That don't signify. I told you, your pa, he didn't want you and your sister mixing with that side of my family. Maybe he was right and maybe not. That don't matter. What matters now is getting some people here fast to help us free the child.'

'You want I should take the mare and ride wherever 'tis?'

'That's the idea. Listen, it's an easy enough ride and you should be there before midday. You've to ride north to the Niobrara River. You cross it at the ford, you know where I mean?'

'Sure I do.'

'Well then, once you've crossed it, you turn east, that's heading towards where the sun rises, and just ride alongside the river. After ten or twelve miles, you'll come to what they call the Great Sioux Reservation. That part, where first you arrive, is where the Santee Sioux have their villages. Leastways, that's what the white men call them. They calls themselves the Isanyathi. When you get there, you've to find the chief, Tamela Pashme. He's my uncle.'

'Your uncle? What can you mean?'

'We don't have time for this. I told you yesterday, if you recollect, that my mother was born and raised with the Sioux? She went off with my granma and lived with the white folk, but her brother never did. He was the chief's son, the old chief, Wabasha. He's your kin as well, and you'd do well to remember it. Now eat, while I get on and tack up the horse. You

73

tell my uncle everything and tell him we need his help desperate sore.'

Dave Jackson was waiting for everybody to leave the ranch in the early morning, so that he could move in and steal whatever he could lay his hands on. He wasn't worried about just what that might be, whether it was cash money or jewellery, firearms or anything else that could be sold to provide him with a little money. It was after the hands had left for work and only the McDonalds and their trail boss were left that Jackson saw an amazing sight. It was Chris Rigby, walking across the yard, hand in hand with a young boy. At least, he assumed that it was a boy, for the slight figure was clad in pants and a shirt. Looking closer though, he saw that the hair was long and braided, which suggested that it might really be a girl child. Not that it mattered which, here was a chance to do an ill turn to the McDonalds and get his own back for Andrew McDonald's summary dismissal of him the day before. More than that, this might also be what he needed to bring him a tidy sum of money. The day was looking up.

As soon as Josephine McDonald woke, she glanced at once over to the other bed and was relieved to find that the child was just laying there, looking up at the ceiling. Climbing out of bed, Josephine went over to a dresser and, opening a drawer, she selected some clothes. Elizabeth said, 'Whose room is this?'

'It was my son's,' replied the other, shortly.

'Is he grown up now?'

'No, he never growed up. Here, you can't walk around in your nightgown. See if these clothes'll fit you.'

The child showed no inclination to get dressed immediately, saying, 'He never grew up? You mean he. . . ?'

'Yes, he died. He was about your age. Here, there's some pants and a shirt. If they don't fit you, well it'll only be for a short spell. Your ma will be coming by soon enough and taking you back home again. Come, be a good girl and get dressed. We can have some breakfast.'

Although she was not a sentimental woman, Josephine had left Billy's room just as it had been on the day of his death, eleven years ago. From time to time, she came in here and just sat and thought about her son. The complications after his birth had meant that there would be no more children and so her firstborn and only child meant more to her than anything in the world. When he took ill with the ague and died after a short illness, at just twelve years of age, Josephine had thought that her entire world would come to an end. That's not really how it works though; it is only in cheap novelettes that folk die of grief.

As Elizabeth removed her nightgown and tried on

75

Billy's clothes, Josephine McDonald looked away, allowing the girl some modesty. Her eyes fell on the dresser, where a row of yellow-jacketed Tauchnitz editions of various classic novels resided. Billy had been a great one for reading; proper books, that is. No dime novels for him! Where he had got his brains was something of a mystery, for she and her husband had little in the way of formal education. Still, there it was. The child had been sharp as a lancet and already, before his thirteenth birthday, his parents were thinking about where he would eventually go to college. It was the unbearable thought of leaving the home where her son had been raised that, as much as anything, caused Josephine to take such extreme measures to hang on to the place.

'You look sad,' said Elizabeth, who was now dressed, 'Are you thinking about your boy?'

'I was, yes. Those britches are a little on the long side. Here, let me roll them up for you.' She knelt at the girl's feet and fiddled with the pants' legs until they looked a little more presentable. 'There,' she said, 'that's better. I guess you'll be wanting something to eat?'

At that moment, there came a knock on the door. Chris Rigby poked his head around the door and said, 'Begging your pardon, ma'am, but your husband begs the favour of a word before he rides down to see to some work.'

Josephine turned to the little girl and said, 'Listen,

76

honey, I have to go and see about something. Go with this young man and he'll see you fed and watered.'

Chris smiled at Elizabeth and said, 'Why, I took you for a boy! Are you really a girl?' The child smiled at him. For all that it had been a disconcerting experience to be plucked from her home in the middle of the night, she seemed to sense that none of those at the ranch meant her any harm and they were so agreeable towards her that the episode had turned into something of an adventure. It had also served to take her mind, however temporarily, from the bereavement that she had suffered. She went off with Chris Rigby, who led her by the hand across the yard, while Josephine McDonald went off in search of her husband.

Dave Jackson's first thought on catching sight of the child was that this must be some relative of the McDonalds; no doubt some little nephew or niece that they were fond of, although he did not recollect ever seeing a little'un about the place or hearing tell of any such family member. Still, what else could this be? Here was the perfect way to be revenged upon his former boss. What if he snatched and harmed this child? Surely that would cause grief to the McDonalds? Hot on the heels of this thought, came another. Away over in the Indian Nations, there were cat houses where young girls were at a very high premium. He had availed himself of the services of such places in the past. He seemed to recall that there was a constant desire for girls who had never before lain with a man. The rumour was that fabulous sums of money changed hand for such commodities. Here, unless his eyes played him false, was a little girl who could fetch a good amount in this trade.

From what Jackson could see, there was nobody else about now other than the McDonalds, Jeff Rigby and the child. Rigby had taken the girl to the hut near the cabins, which served as a canteen for the ranch. All he need do was to take her and ride hell for leather west until he reached the territories.

Although they were currently in the doldrums as far as work went, the McDonalds' ranch was built to accommodate dozens of men when it was working at full capacity. Four bunkhouses contained cots for twenty men each and opposite them was a low building with a stove and trestle tables, where the cowboys could eat. It was to this building that the trail boss took little Elizabeth Hogan that morning. She was a perky little thing, he thought, as he got her to sit down while he stirred up the fire in the stove and asked, 'Pancakes alright for you? You allowed coffee?'

'Of course I'm allowed coffee! I'm nearly twelve.'

Rigby smiled. Entertaining a little girl in this way was certainly a change from his usual duties. He felt called upon to offer some slight apology for seizing this child the night before and said, 'I'm right sorry about detaining you like this. You must think we're a regular set of villains.'

'Oh no,' said Elizabeth seriously, 'You all seem right nice. That lady's very sad, ain't she?'

'Mrs McDonald?' asked Rigby in surprise. He'd had the rough edge of Josephine McDonald's tongue too often in the past to have noticed any sadness about her. He said vaguely, 'It may be so.' He turned to busy himself with preparing breakfast for the guest and so had his back to the door when Dave Jackson entered quietly.

Elizabeth had no reason to suspect that the man who walked through the door was anything other than somebody else working on the ranch. She nodded politely to him and watched as he walked across the room towards Chris Rigby, who was clattering about with pans, which masked the sound of Jackson's footsteps. When he reached the man setting a pan on the stove, in readiness for making pancakes, Jackson drew a wickedly sharp knife from a sheath that was attached to his belt at the back, out of sight under his jacket. Then he said, 'Hey, Rigby!'

When the trail boss turned around in surprise, Jackson plunged the knife between Rigby's ribs, on the left-hand side. For a moment, there was a look of anger in his victim's face, as though he were about to fight back or perhaps pluck out the knife. When a man's heart has been carved nearly in half though there is little to be done and so, without further ado,

79

Chris Rigby dropped to the floor and died. The girl witnessed all this without much realizing what was going on. She had never seen any deliberate act of violence in the whole course of her life and thought for a moment that the men were just fooling around. It was not until the nice man who offered to make her pancakes fell down on the floor that she knew that something terrible had happened. At that point, she got to her feet and made for the door, but Jackson was after her in a flash, saying in a soft, but deadly voice, 'Oh no you don't!'

Sometimes in nightmares, Elizabeth Hogan had been rooted to the spot in the face of some oncoming terror and when she had tried to scream, only an inaudible, strangled noise had been able to escape from her throat. She felt exactly the same now, because she wanted to scream, was trying to scream, but nothing came out. She was at that level of terror that has an almost paralysing effect on a body. It was quite a different feeling from the previous night, when those three figures had appeared out of nowhere. She had somehow sensed on that occasion that these were not bad people and that had ameliorated the fear that had gripped her. Now, the case was wholly altered. She knew that she was in the presence of evil and the knowledge was so shockingly frightening that there was nothing she could say or do.

Grabbing the girl with one hand, Jackson replaced

the gory, dripping knife in its sheath with the other and then drew the pistol at his hip, cocking it with his thumb as he did so. A quick glance out of the door assured him that there was nobody around. It would have been all the worse for that person, if there had been. He said quietly to the child whose arm he was gripping tightly, 'You make so much as a peep and it's all up with you, you hear what I tell you? You cry out and before God, I'll cut out your tongue.'

Sweeping the terrified child up into his arms, Dave Jackson set off at an easy run, up the slope to the trees where his horse was tethered. He felt a savage exultation, for he had surely had his own back on that Andrew McDonald. Not only had he deprived him of a first-class trail boss, he had also carried away a child who was probably a favoured relative of the McDonalds. Best of all, he now had his road stake. Unless he was very much mistaken, this little girl would fetch several hundred dollars once he delivered her to one of the larger brothels in the Indian Territories.

CHAPTER 5

Three years after the end of the War Between the States, the government in Washington signed a treaty that, it was hoped, would bring a final end to the Indian 'problem', in particular Red Cloud's war, known sometimes as the Powder River War. The Treaty of Fort Laramie, signed at that location on 29 April 1868, set aside a vast tract of land in Dakota and Nebraska, including the Black Hills, which was to become the possession of the Sioux nation in perpetuity. The Black Hills were especially important to the Lakota, a branch of the Sioux, as they were believed by them to be holy. The treaty that promised all this to the Indians lasted just six years. In 1874 a mineral survey team operating on behalf of the government found that the Black Hills of south Dakota contained huge quantities of gold. It was perhaps inevitable that a gold rush would follow this discovery. The gold on the bluff on the Hogans' land was an outlying vein from these same huge deposits.

To begin with, the US army tried to keep the prospectors out of the Black Hills. Then they began to drive back the Indians, who were intent on killing those who were profaning their most sacred site. In Washington, the government could see clear advantages in a steady flow of gold from south Dakota and thought that this would stimulate the economy generally, which was likely enough true. Using the outraged reaction of the Lakota-Sioux as a pretext, Washington tore up the Treaty of Fort Laramie and carved up the Sioux Reservation into smaller parcels of land, none of which were sufficiently large in size for the inhabitants to live by either hunting or farming. Instead, the Sioux became increasingly dependent on the rations handed out by the Indian Agency. Before this state of affairs was reached, of course, there took place the Great Sioux War of 1876.

The desecration, as they saw it, of the Black Hills by the white men digging for gold served as a rallying cry for the Sioux, who launched a heroic, but futile, war to drive the white men from their lands. The Indians won a few famous victories, most notably at the Battle of the Little Bighorn when better than two hundred and fifty troopers of the 7th cavalry were massacred, but the result of the war itself was never in doubt for a moment. By April 1877, at the time that Andrew McDonald was trying to wrest control of the bluff on the Hogans' land from them, the fighting had more or less come to an end. On the 23rd of that month, an aide to General Crooke, one of those most vigorous in prosecuting the war against the Lakota-Sioux, wrote to a friend, saying, 'I am now fully satisfied that the great Sioux war is ended.' So it proved, for there was to be no more serious fighting after that time, merely a few desultory skirmishes.

By all of which, it will be correctly gauged that this was not the best of times for a young boy who had not even begun to shave to be riding into the Niobrara Reservation, where feelings about the late war were exceedingly strong. Zachariah Hogan, though, was a young man who knew his duty and if his mother said that this was the correct course of action to save the life of his little sister, then this was what he would do.

Although the fighting of the previous year had taken place at times pretty near their home, the Hogans had seen little of it. Every so often in the summer of 1876, they had seen bands of cavalry passing through, heading north towards the Sioux lands. That had been the sum total of their involvement though. If Melanie Hogan, whose own mother had been born and raised among the Sioux, had any ideas on the subject, perhaps conflicts of loyalty between her allegiance to her own race and that of the Indians, she took care to keep such things to herself. Her husband's ideas on the matter of the proper place of Indians in a civilized, white nation were orthodox in the extreme, and as far as Melanie was concerned her husband was the head of the family and his views were to be endorsed without question.

As Zachariah rode north that morning, he was turning over in his head the facts that had recently come to light regarding his mother's, and by extension his own, ancestry. His own views on Indians were pretty much as one might expect from a white youth of that time and place. He had always regarded the Sioux as bloodthirsty savages who threatened the very existence of his own nation. That his mother had been raised in part by Indians and that his own grandma, whom he had never met in the flesh. was next door to being completely Indian herself, were strange and disconcerting propositions.

The track led north, in the general direction of the Black Hills. After a few miles, Zac came to the Niobrara River, which was at that point broad, shallow and easily forded. After crossing the river, he turned to the right, as his mother had instructed him to do, and rode along the bank towards the reservation of the Santee Sioux. Knowing the urgency of his mission, the boy was tempted to race at top speed, but had to make a conscious effort not to spur on the mare to a frantic gallop. It would help nobody if the beast took a tumble and broke a leg! There was no track alongside the Niobrara; it was all rough and uneven ground, littered with stones and rocks. For most of the time, Zac proceeded at a lively trot, speeding up to a canter when there were clear, smooth stretches of grassland.

Fifteen miles does not sound any great distance to travel, but when you have just lately lost one family member and the life of another hangs in the balance, the temptation to hurry and fetch whatever help might be available is nigh-on irresistible. Under those circumstances, it was not a bit surprising that Zachariah was travelling faster than was wise or desirable and that, as a direct consequence, his horse put her hoof into a prairie dog hole and fell hard, pitching her rider off in a most ignominious fashion. At first, Zac was afraid that the creature might have broken a leg in the fall, which would have been a dreadful thing. This swiftly proved not to be the case, for she leapt nimbly to her feet and took off across the open grassland, without seemingly giving a thought to her supposed owner.

Zachariah Hogan jumped to his feet and called after his treacherous mount, but to no avail. He stood there in despair. Had he been just a very little bit younger, the boy might well have burst into tears of vexation, but as it was he simply stood there, without the faintest idea of what he should next do. It was in this attitude that he caught sight of a party of horsemen riding down upon him from the gently sloping ridge of land to his left. He wasn't all that well up on the customs of Indian tribes, but Zac could not help but notice that these ten or twelve fellows all seemed to be carrying bows and lances. They looked, to his untutored eye, like men who were riding to war.

After she had finished conferring with her husband, Josephine McDonald went off to find her young guest. Although Chris Rigby had always struck her as a pleasant and God-fearing young man, she was uneasily conscious of the impropriety of leaving a young girl child in the charge of a single, unmarried man. Besides which, she had enjoyed the child's company and wished to make perfectly sure that little Elizabeth fully understood that she was in no sort of danger from them and that she would be returning to her mother and brother that very day. Her husband was walking around the ranch, glancing anxiously to the south, so that as soon as Mrs Hogan showed up, they could conclude their business with as much goodwill as was possible, given the unfortunate circumstances. The first intimation he had that his carefully laid plan might be about to miscarry was when he heard a piercing shriek from the direction of the bunkhouses. He ran as fast as he could to see what was amiss, to find his wife standing in the doorway of the canteen. She was deathly white, and for a moment McDonald thought that she had been hurt. He said, 'For God's sake, what ails you?' She gestured wordlessly towards the interior of the hut where the hands ate their meals.

He'd seen dead men before, those who had been shot, but never in all his born days had Andrew McDonald seen a man who had been knifed to death. He would not have conceived it possible that one body could contain so much blood. Chris Rigby lay in an enormous pool of his own blood, but that was not the limit of it, for this puddle or pool had run along the uneven, clay floor, until it reached the nearest wall. It put McDonald in mind of a large pot of paint that might have been tipped out. Gingerly, tiptoeing delicately through the gore, Andrew McDonald made his way to where his trail boss lay. It was clear that there was nothing to be done for the man; he lay there stone dead, with his eyes wide open and staring sightlessly at the grimy ceiling. From behind him, McDonald's wife said in an urgent and panic-stricken voice, 'Where's that child?'

Josephine's words recalled McDonald to life and he spun around, scanning the room closely to see if little Elizabeth Hogan was hiding in some corner. She wasn't. He said, 'You take the bunkhouses, I'll search the yard.'

'You think she might have done this?' asked Josephine in a horrified tone, 'What's happened?'

'No child did this thing. There's evil at work here.'

The man and woman raced off to try and find where the little girl might be. It was to no avail; there was not the slightest trace of Elizabeth and no sign to indicate where she gone or been taken. The death of Chris Rigby had shaken them both, but the realization that a child in their safekeeping had somehow been lost was of far greater import. It is to the credit of both Andrew and Josephine McDonald that in their anxiety about the girl's disappearance they had both forgotten entirely that she meant the saving of their livelihood and home.

'What's become of her, Andrew?' asked Josephine, when they had looked all around their property, 'Has she run off or what?'

'Damned if I know. I'll ride out, look about a bit. She can't have got far, how long since you saw her head off to the canteen with Rigby?'

'It can't be above ten minutes at most. Find her, Andrew. That poor little thing. What were we about, taking her from her home like that?'

Andrew McDonald looked at his wife and said shortly, 'You'll recollect that it was your idea.' Then he went off to saddle up and go off to hunt for the missing child.

Although she had despatched her son to seek help from her Indian kin, Melanie did not really believe that Elizabeth would have come to harm. Andrew McDonald might be a greedy and unscrupulous landowner, but from all that she was able to collect, neither he nor his wife were killers. True, they were connected in some fashion with the death of her husband, but shooting a grown man was in a different class to hurting a little girl. After thinking the matter over carefully, she had come to the conclusion that taking her daughter was only a gambit to increase their bargaining power, Melanie did not really apprehend any danger for the girl. She was, for all that, mightily aggrieved about the whole thing and was determined to show the McDonalds just how ticked off she was.

When Melanie had lived for those two years in the village of the Santee Sioux, she acquired a powerfully strong reputation for two things. One was a violent and intractable disposition, which manifested itself in a fiery temper and willingness to fight any comer if she felt herself wronged or cheated. Although the Indians had no sort of race prejudice against white people and would later be quite content for Melanie's half-breed uncle to lead the tribe, they found the behaviour of the little white girl faintly shocking. She romped with the boys, fought them, competed in their games on equal terms and was even better than any of them at some of their favoured pastimes. All of which led naturally to the other thing for which the young girl became renowned: skill with a bow and arrow.

While the other girls her age were fooling around with looms or learning to cook, Melanie was out with the boys; first playing at hunting and then, when she had the skill, actually tracking down and killing game. Once they realized that here was a girl who could hold her own, the boys stopped trying to drive the white girl from their activities and grudgingly accepted her into their world. At first, the bows they used were no more than springy saplings, but later they began to make more reliable weapons under the guidance of older men of the tribe. The old men too tolerated Melanie's presence and allowed her to learn the craft of bow-making, a very rare thing for any female to study.

Melanie Hogan picked up the bow that she had fashioned when she had been just eleven years of age. It was a composite of buffalo horn and leather. The string had perished; it was originally made from the innards of the same buffalo whose horn had been used. Although a little smaller than the bows carried by grown-up warriors, it was perfectly adequate for the use of a woman or child. She hunted around for some twine, which she soon unearthed. It would hardly matter if the string was of hemp rather than animal guts.

After restringing the bow, Melanie Hogan went outside and loosed off a few of the shafts that she had stored away during her married life. Her aim was as unerring as ever it had been. She used as a target the nearest fencepost and found that after adjusting for the differing tension that a length of cord gave, as opposed to a narrow strip of intestine, she was as accurate with the bow as she had been as a child.

Going back into the house, she threaded the sheath of her knife through one of Caleb's belts and fastened it around her waist. The bow she slung across her back and the half dozen flint-tipped arrows she carried in her hand. Thus prepared, she set off on foot for the McDonald ranch, where she confidently expected to find her daughter. Sending Zachariah off to fetch aid from her people had been, as much as anything, a device to put the boy out of reach of harm. Not but that it would be handy to have a little help in this present endeavour. Melanie doubted though that she would need it. She felt that cold, burning rage that she had spent so much of her adult life suppressing. She guessed that she would have settled matters before any of the Santee Sioux arrived on the scene.

After having hoisted her onto the saddle in front of him, Dave Jackson said to the little girl in a low and menacing voice, 'You cause me a speck o' trouble and I'll cut your throat, you hear what I tell you?'

Elizabeth nodded dumbly, so terrified that she could scarcely breathe. She whispered, 'Don't hurt me, sir.'

'Nobody goin' to get hurt, not so long as you do as I bid you.'

Once he was safely in the saddle himself, Jackson set his mount cantering off, heading east. He meant to put as much distance between him and the

McDonald ranch as ever he could. As he rode along, he gloated over the agony that he would be causing the McDonalds by taking away this child and selling her into a life of prostitution. He expected to raise a tidy sum from the projected transaction in the Indian Nations, but it was relishing the harm that he was doing to another that sustained Dave Jackson.

Elizabeth said, 'Please sir, where are we going?'

'Don't you trouble your head about that. Just you make sure to do as I say and things'll turn out a sight easier.'

After they had been cantering for fifteen or twenty minutes, Jackson thought that it would do no harm to ease up the pace a little. He allowed the horse to slow down to a trot for a while. He said to the child, 'We'll not be stopping for aught until late afternoon, so if you're minded to tell me that you're hungry, thirsty, sore, tired or I don't know what-all else, then you needn't trouble to speak. Is that plain?'

'Yes sir.'

Something about the girl's meekness irritated Dave Jackson and he said, 'You've no need to call me "sir". Dave's my name or Jackson, if you'd rather.'

There was no answer and so he gave up and focused his mind once more on having got one over on Andrew McDonald for having given him his marching orders.

Elizabeth Hogan might have been just eleven years old and exceedingly young for her age, but she was

93

no fool. She possessed a kind of extra sense when it came to people, one that enabled her to feel almost immediately if the person she was with was decent and good or not to be trusted. This was odd, because her life had been pretty sheltered and she had hardly had much opportunity for meeting bad men and women. Nevertheless, just as she had felt instinctively that the McDonalds and their trail boss were essentially kind and right-thinking individuals, so too did she somehow realize that the man upon whose horse she was now travelling was of an altogether different stamp. The ill nature of the man radiated off him and little Elizabeth could almost feel it. She knew that she was in mortal peril from this man and his plans and that if she did not find a way of escaping from his clutches, then something terrible was going to happen to her. Howsoever, there seemed to be no present prospect of removing herself from him and so, at least for the moment, all she could do was watch and wait.

It had now been well over twelve hours since Elizabeth had eaten and she was beginning to feel distinctly hungry. She had, after all, not had a morsel of food since supper at seven the previous evening. She dared not ask though when they might be stopping for food. Had she but known it, her captor was in far worse case than she. He had not had a bite to eat since the previous morning's breakfast, having spent the whole of the last twenty-four hours crouched in that copse that overlooked the McDonalds' ranch.

After they had been riding for what seemed to Elizabeth ages, but was in fact only about an hour and a half, Jackson reined in as they came upon an isolated farmhouse. It was a cheerful-looking place, white-painted and with green window frames. He said, 'I'm going to have words with whosoever lives here. You sit tight and don't even think of running.' He trotted the horse on until they were only a dozen yards from the door of the house.

Jumping down nimbly, Dave Jackson strode up to the farmhouse door and rapped smartly upon it with his knuckles. After a space, a pleasant-looking woman of about thirty-five or forty years of age opened the door. She smiled and said, 'A very good morning to you, sir. How may I help you?'

'Truth to tell, ma'am, I was hoping to beg the favour of a word with your husband.'

'I'm afraid that won't answer. He's away over yonder in town. Can I help at all?'

'Why, it may be so,' said Jackson in an agreeable tone of voice, 'Are you alone here?'

'That I am.'

'Thank you.' Without any further ado, Dave Jackson swung a punch at the woman's face. This had the effect of making her stagger back and clutch at the doorpost. He followed this first assault up with a flurry of further blows to her face and head. Then, when she collapsed to the ground, he commenced to kick her a few times, to ensure that she stayed down. Then, satisfied presumably that she was quite out of the reckoning, Jackson stepped over her prone body and entered the house.

The sight of such sudden and wholly unprovoked violence caused Elizabeth's heart to pound and for a moment or two she found that she had forgotten to breathe. Her immediate impulse was to flee such a terrible scene, but she knew that a man on horseback would have no difficulty in running her to ground, were she to do so. The only option seemed to be to sit there on the horse and see what next developed. She hadn't long to wait.

After no more than a minute or two, the man who had taken her prisoner came out of the farmhouse, carrying a pink and white gingham tablecloth that was being used to hold a number of bulky items. As he passed the woman whom he had knocked to the ground, she made as if to rise and the man lashed out at her savagely with his boot, sending her sprawling again. Then he marched up to the horse and handed Elizabeth the tablecloth and its contents, saying, 'Here, take a hold of this. And mind you don't let it fall, or it'll be the worse for you!'

As soon as he was in the saddle, Dave Jackson spurred his mount into a canter and they swept away from the house he had lately raided for provisions. Elizabeth clutched the front of the saddle and shrank in horror from the hand that held her safe and steady. The evil that earlier, in her imagination, had come off the man behind her like a mist, now seemed a positive force, as though she were burning in the rays of another sun. She did not know what was to become of her and wondered if she would be able to hold back from screaming in terror or going mad.

They travelled on at a fair speed for twenty minutes or half an hour, before Jackson slowed the horse to a trot and then a walk. He said, 'Well child, I can't speak for you, but I'm fair famished. What say we halt for a picnic meal and eat up some them vittles as I acquired back there?'

'That lady never did you any harm,' said Elizabeth, 'How could you use her so?'

'She never did me no good as I know of neither,' replied Jackson, giving a snort of amusement at his wit, 'but that's nothing to the purpose. You hungry or what?'

'I guess.'

They ate by the side of the track, with Jackson keeping a wary eye out, all around him. He introduced himself again to the frightened girl, telling her that she could just call him 'Dave' and enquiring her own name. She said, 'I'm called Elizabeth Hogan.' On hearing the name, he gave a start, realizing all of a sudden that this was most probably the daughter of the man he had accidentally killed a short while ago. It felt strange to be breaking bread with her now. Like many bad men, Jackson had a strong streak of superstition running through him and when he found out who it was he was carrying off to a life of degradation and near-slavery, he was seized by a dread fear. To cover up his anxiety, he said gruffly, 'You do just as I bid you, then you and me'll get along just fine. But I tell you straight, I'm the very devil if I'm crossed. You understand that?'

'I understand,' said the girl softly, 'I know what you're like.'

Jackson shot her a look, to see if she was sassing him, but the child's face was perfectly respectful and serious. He saw that she had hardly touched the bread, cheese and cold meat that he had stolen from the kitchen of the farmhouse he had looted. He said, 'What's the matter with you? Why aren't you eating?'

'It don't seem right, somehow. Not after what you did that lady.'

This criticism enraged Jackson and he said harshly, 'Let's you and me rightly understand each other. I'll do whatever's needful to survive and if that means taking food without the owner's leave, then so be it. I don't look for a child to catch me up on it neither. Just you eat up, now. I don't aim to arrive where we're going with you looking as thin as a rake and pale as a hant. That won't do.'

'Where are we going?' asked Elizabeth, taking a small piece of cheese and placing it in her mouth to placate him. 'I don't mind that you tell me why you've took me.'

'Well, that's by way of being a long tale and I don't see a need to tell it now. Let's just say that I mistook you for another. Not that it matters none. We'll be on the road for three or four days and then we'll get where we're headin'. There, that enough information for you?'

Elizabeth Hogan shrugged. What was plain as the nose on her face was that she had become entangled with a very bad man, one who might not even shrink from murder. Innocent and young she might be, but she knew that it wouldn't do to get cross-wise to this fellow. Equally, nothing pleasant was likely to be awaiting her at journey's end. There was nothing for it but to keep quiet for the time being and then see if any opportunity presented itself along the way, either to escape from 'Dave' or, if necessary to do him some mischief. Gentle as she was, there were times when the use of violence was justified and Elizabeth had an idea that this was one of those rare occasions.

CHAPTER 6

The troop of riders flowed down from the higher ground as smoothly as a stream of water and then circled Zachariah, watching him the while. He observed that they appeared to be armed not with guns, but more traditional weapons, such as lances and bows. Without a word of command, all the warriors reined in their mounts and stood round him, presumably waiting for Zachariah to say or do something. He supposed on one level that he might be in some kind of danger, but the chief emotion he felt was embarrassment; fifteen or so young men, all staring at him and expecting him to do the Lord knows what. One of the riders lowered his lance until the point was aiming straight at Zachariah's breast and then walked his horse forward, not halting until the sharp tip of the spear was no more than a foot from Zac.

It was obvious that something would have to be said and so the awkward white youth cleared his throat and announced, 'I don't know how far I am from the Santee Sioux village, but I'm looking for them. I've kin there, a man called Tamela Pashme.' He wondered if he was pronouncing the name correctly, for the expressionless men surrounding him gave no indication that his words conveyed anything in particular to them. Feeling a little desperate now and keenly aware of the passage of time and the need to fetch aid for his sister as soon as might be, Zachariah continued, addressing his question directly to the rider who had his lance only a few inches from his heart, 'Are you folk Isanyathi?'

'Isanyathi,' said the rider in front of Zac, altering the stress of the syllables slightly.

'Is that how you say it?' asked Zac. 'Well then, that's who I'm a-looking for. An uncle o' mine is in charge of 'em, seemingly. Fellow by the name of Tamela Pashme. Happen you know him?'

The young man in front of him stared for a moment and then, to Zachariah's great surprise and immense relief, his immobile face split into a wide smile. The rider said something to the other men, who also appeared to relax a little and also started to exchange comments among themselves. The man who had the lance pointing at Zac's chest raised it and secured it to his saddle somehow. Then he dismounted and walked up to Zachariah, his white teeth signalling nothing but goodwill. He said, 'We're kin, you and me. You must be my cousin.'

This was such a surprising turn of events that Zachariah simply stood gaping at the man, who could have been no more than four or five years older than he. He said, 'Cousins? How come?'

'Your mother is the daughter of Tamela Pashme's sister, is it not so?'

Zac scratched his head thoughtfully, wishing that he'd listened a little more closely to what his mother had told him of her family history. Then he said slowly, 'Well, my ma told me that Tamela Pashme is her uncle, so yes, I reckon it might be as you say.'

'Tamela Pashme is my mother's father,' said the Indian triumphantly. 'We are cousins indeed.'

For want of anything else to say, Zachariah remarked vaguely, 'You speak good English,' and then immediately regretted it, thinking that it might sound as though he thought that Indians were all unlettered savages. 'I didn't mean nothing. Just that you speak like me.'

'I went to a mission school. And my aunt, she always said how I should learn the white man's ways.' Now it was the turn of the young Indian brave to feel a little abashed, for he was afraid that the white boy would be offended at his reference to 'white man's ways'. He continued, 'She said that I was half white and so I should be able to speak like a white man, as well as a Sioux.'

'My ma, I guess that would be your aunt's daughter, she sent me here to ask for help. My sister, she's been taken by bad men and Ma said that you folk'd lend a hand.'

'Your sister must be my cousin too. The village is not far. Jump up with me and we'll be there in no time.'

It took little time to reach the village. Zachariah had never seen an Indian village before and looked around him in frank curiosity. There were dozens of tents, what would, he supposed, be called tepees. Everybody seemed very busy, but when once they caught sight of a white person entering their camp, work was suspended and people drifted over to see what was what. Maybe, thought Zac, they think I'm a prisoner or something. When he got down, people at first moved back, as though they were unsure of him. Then the crowd parted and a squaw came forward with the evident intention of greeting him. She was dressed exactly like all the other women and her skin was certainly no paler, but there was something quite extraordinary about her hair, which was sun-bleached to the colour of ripe wheat. Zac couldn't help staring at this apparition in astonishment, forgetting his manners and making no attempt to greet the woman.

'What ails you boy, cat got your tongue?'

'I'm sorry, ma'am, I was thinking as you might be somebody I came to see. My mother's called Melanie Hogan.'

The woman, whose age Zachariah could not begin to gauge, snorted and said, 'Hogan indeed! Well well, we'll let that pass. You must be my grandson. I ain't seen you since you was a babe in arms. You've growed tall and strong enough. Come, give your grandma a kiss.'

Hesitantly, Zac went forward and kissed his grandmother's leathery cheek. She grasped his arm to detain him for a moment, peering hard at his face and saying, 'I'd o' come by and visited you know, if only your ma had o' said it would be fine. But your pa, he wouldn't have it.'

Not wanting to hear any criticism of his father and suddenly recollecting the dreadful fact that he was dead, Zachariah said, 'My father was killed just lately. Now my sister's gone and we need help in getting her back again.'

'Why didn't you say so before, boy?' said his grandmother. She shouted at the young man upon whose horse Zac had ridden into the camp, 'Hey, you there, shake a leg. My daughter, as is your own aunt, needs help. Go see your grandfather and get him moving.' She turned to Zac and said, the pride unmistakable, 'I dare say you heard that my brother's the chief o' the whole tribe? Ain't that something?'

It was plain from the way that folk in the village minded her that Zachariah's grandmother was a person of some consequence. She threaded her way through the tents, shooing some children aside here

104

and chiding grown women for not moving aside swiftly enough. As she walked, she remarked to Zac, 'Those boys'll take a good hour to get ready. Don't you worry none though, my brother'll see things right. You can come and have a bite to eat with me, while you're a-waitin'. Tell me about my family that I've not seen for these many years.' They reached a tepee, at which the woman halted and then bent down to lift up a flap, gesturing for Zachariah to enter before her.

Andrew McDonald returned after twenty minutes, having galloped around the perimeter area surrounding his ranch. There was no sign of the missing child. Josephine rushed up to him, saying, 'What can have become of her? And who killed Rigby?'

Grim-faced and pale, McDonald replied, 'I've a notion that I know the answer to both them questions. You know I threw out that drunken fool Jackson, after he shot Caleb Hogan? He's a mean one. I reckon as he's decided to do us a bad turn in return. Maybe he thinks the child is something to do with us. And there was no love 'tween him and Chris Rigby. Mark my words, Jackson's at the bottom of this.'

'Lord a-mercy, what are we to do? Is there no clue which way that villain's gone?'

Andrew McDonald shook his head in despair and said, 'It'd need an Indian tracker to find his trail. It's beyond me. The best I can do is round up the boys and set them out searching. I'm greatly afeared though as Jackson will have harmed the child, just to cause us anguish.'

At these words, Josephine felt as though an icy hand had clutched at her heart. She repented fully and absolutely of having been the motive power behind the snatching of the little girl and felt such guilt and shame as could hardly be imagined. She said, 'I must hunt for that poor little creature too. This is all my fault.' Her husband said nothing, but she could see in his eyes that he was thinking exactly the same thing. She exclaimed, 'Mother of God, Andrew, don't look at me so! I meant no harm to her, you know that.'

McDonald shook his head sombrely and said, 'Makes no odds what we did and didn't mean. Fact is, we're put that child in harm's way and if aught happens to her, I'll never forgive myself.' He did not need to add, 'or you'; Josephine could see in his face what he was thinking.

McDonald dismounted and came over to his wife. He said, 'I don't lay this charge on you, Josephine. God knows we were both desperate enough to save our home and this is the result.'

Before she was able to frame an adequate answer, there came a rushing, whistling noise and something flashed past, real low. Andrew McDonald gave a cry of pain and clapped both hands to his buttocks.

106

When he brought one hand up again, it was stained with blood. At the same moment, Josephine saw what had flown past her. It had stuck in the ground some six feet away and from the look of it, could only be an Indian arrow.

Melanie was good and mad, but not really fearing that any mischief had befallen her daughter. She guessed, quite correctly, that this was just some way of putting the bite on her to agree to a disadvantageous deal regarding her land. She had no reason to suppose either of the McDonalds to be wicked or cruel, they were just determined as anything to steal the gold that was on her land. Thinking about this made her so angry that she could hardly breathe and so Melanie sat down for a minute, until she had calmed down somewhat. And all this, she thought wrathfully, for gold! Her dear husband dead and her daughter taken from her, just so these worthless wretches could add to their own not inconsiderable fortune! Well, they would rue the day that they had started out down this road, that was for certain-sure. She, Melanie Hogan, would show them the error of their ways and see to it that they remembered to their dying days what a terrible mistake they had made in crossing her path.

It took the better part of two hours to reach the edge of the McDonalds' ranch and Melanie took care not to be seen by anybody as she made her way there. She didn't think that there'd be many tears shed locally if anything unpleasant befell Andrew McDonald, but there was no percentage in advertising what she was about. When she reached the rise of ground with a copse at the top, where Dave Jackson had spent the night spying on the McDonalds, Melanie walked up and then, as she neared the crest, fell to her knees and began crawling. She'd no wish to find herself silhouetted against the skyline when she reached the top.

The object of the exercise was, to Melanie, twofold. On the one hand, she intended to take her little daughter home that day. Then again, she proposed to deliver such a sharp lesson to Andrew McDonald that he would wake up screaming from his sleep ten years from now, when he recalled how he had been foolish enough to cross Melanie Hogan and fool around with her child.

From the trees, there was a perfect view down to the ranch house and the yard around it. Melanie could see Andrew McDonald, seated on a horse and exchanging words with his wife. She could not, at this range, hear what was being said, but she guessed by the expressions on their faces that they were talking about something serious. There was no sign of Elizabeth. Wriggling forward on her belly, Melanie stopped at a tree and then stood up behind it, out of sight of anybody below. Then she took the bow slung across her back and fitted one of the arrows that she was holding carefully to the string. She was about sixty yards from the two figures. There was no wind to speak of and so that wasn't a problem. The only thing that could go wrong was that she might inadvertently kill one of the McDonalds. This did not strike Melanie Hogan as something that needed to be factored into her decision. She intended to punish the man standing there talking to his wife, and if he died of it then so be it.

Taking very careful aim at Andrew McDonald's buttocks, Melanie let fly. From this angle, she hoped that the arrow would slice through the fat of his legs, without causing any great injury. If a stray gust of wind sent her arrow straight into his privates though, she would not grieve. As it was, the shot was as clean as could be, with the flint-tipped arrow flying straight and true, gouging a deep furrow across one of the rancher's buttocks. As soon as she was sure that McDonald was wounded, Melanie stood up and jog-trotted down the slope to where Josephine McDonald was trying to calm her husband and examine the extent and severity of his injury. So occupied were they with this task, that they neither of them heard her approaching and it wasn't until she was standing a few feet away, with her knife drawn, that they became aware of her.

There was, Elizabeth had decided, no point in starving herself, no matter how the vittles had been acquired. She came to this conclusion after watching the man called Dave stuffing his face without a care in the world. If she was going to survive this, then she would at the very least need to feed her body. Because she had led something of a sheltered life, Elizabeth, although on the verge of puberty, knew next to nothing about the world. She was vaguely aware that men were rougher, louder and more dangerous than women, but that was about the sum total of her knowledge on the subject. She knew instinctively that the man sitting a short distance from her and currently gnawing a bone was some sort of threat to her, but beyond the possibility that he would strike her, maybe even shoot her, she didn't know what harm he could do her.

Jackson became aware of the child's scrutiny and looked up, scowling at her fiercely. 'What for are ye starin' at me so?' he enquired pugnaciously, 'Something wrong with the way I look?'

'Sorry. I didn't mean to stare.'

'You'll have to mend your manners where we're headed, child. I'll tell you that for nothing. Sauce won't answer there, you hear what I say?'

Never before in her life had Elizabeth Hogan been accused of 'sauce'. She said, 'Where are we going? I don't recollect that you told me.'

'Well then, we're a-goin' to the Indian Nations.'

'Indian? Is that where they've been fighting?'

'No, not a bit of it. These are the five civilized

110

tribes. They don't go fighting anybody, or leastways if they do it ain't white men. Just scrapping with one another.'

Elizabeth thought this over as she munched a little bread and cheese and then said, 'If'n you let me go now, I wouldn't tell on you. I'd let you get away free.'

Dave Jackson eyed her ironically and replied, 'Well, that's mighty nice of you, but I reckon as I'll keep down the path I planned.'

When the two of them had finished eating, they got back on the horse and set off again. It seemed to the girl that she would either have to escape or perhaps find somebody who would rescue her. The opportunity came after they had been proceeding east for another hour or more.

The track that they were travelling along was not a wide or populous thoroughfare. Indeed, since leaving the ranch, they had so far encountered no other travellers. It was not until an hour after their meal that Jackson and the girl came across anybody else on the road. They were riding across a flat, grassy plain that stretched, featureless and bland, to the horizon. Here and there were small houses and the landscape was punctuated with the occasional culti-vated field, but other than that there was nothing to be see but parched, scrubby grass. Because they could see for several miles ahead of them, Jackson was aware, long before they reached it, of a wagon by the side of the track, around which two figures were fussing and doing something or other. When they were a couple of hundred yards off from this scene, he said to Elizabeth, 'Say one word to those folks and I'll skin you alive. You understand me?'

As they drew closer, it was obvious what was going on. Something was amiss with the cart and the two men were struggling to fix it. Their strength was not sufficient to accomplish the task, however, because the cart needed to be raised so that one man could get underneath and work on the axle. It took the two of them to lift the thing up, meaning that there was a need for a third person to effect the necessary repair. Of course, Dave Jackson knew nothing of this, nor would he have cared much if he had known. He simply wished to pass on without let or hindrance, but it was not to be.

As they approached, one of those fooling around with the wagon stepped out onto the dusty road and hailed them in loud and cheerful voice, crying, 'Say friend, might we ask you to lend a hand here? We need two stout fellows to lift it up while one of us fixes the axle. As you can see, we're a man short for such an operation.'

Two strong urges fought for mastery in Dave Jackson's breast. The first of these impulses was to tell this impertinent man to clear the road and tend to his own affairs, without trying to draw others into his problems. Then again though, Jackson was desirous of making his way to the territories without drawing any undue attention to himself. A surly and uncooperative man, hurrying along with a little girl in front of him on his saddle, might very well be something that could become the object of remark. The last thing he needed was to have some meddlesome fool set up a hue and cry and give his description to the law.

While Jackson hesitated, the man who had asked for assistance said, 'Surely you wouldn't spurn to help a fellow being in his hour of need?'

It was on the tip of Dave Jackson's tongue to tell this importunate individual that he had often spurned to help any number of folk in their hour of need, when the other man who had working on the cart, who had been staring hard at Jackson and his young companion, said, 'I know you. Your name is Jackson and you're a damned villain.'

This was so unexpected that for a moment, tough as he was, Jackson felt as though all the breath had been punched out of his body. The man continued, 'You most likely forgot my face, but I ain't forgot your'n, you bastard.' Then, recollecting himself and seeing that there was a girl of tender years present, he said, 'Beggin' your pardon for the language, little miss.'

'My name's not Jackson. You're making some kind of mistake.'

'You think so?' said the man who had recognized Jackson, coming away from the cart and standing

113

next to the man with whom he had been working, 'You don't recall my face, I'll be bound. I was in a stage, best part of two years since. You and another held it up. Away over yonder in Oklahoma. You shot a woman there, on account of she was too quick in reaching in her bag for the money you demanded we all hand over. Remember now? Memory coming back to you now? You thought she was going for a weapon.'

Dave Jackson said nothing, for his mind was racing frantically, trying to find a way out of this trap. The two men standing before him both had guns at their hips and they both had that indefinable air about them of men who knew how to take care of themselves. This was the devil of business and, for now, Jackson could see no way out of the coils. That was until Elizabeth Hogan piped up and said, 'His name is Jackson and he's stolen me away and is taking me to the Indian Nations. I want to go home.' Then, before Jackson knew what she was about, the child had wriggled free and, dismounting clumsily, had fallen to the ground in a heap.

It didn't look like he would get a better opportunity than this and so before the girl had even hit the dust, Jackson drew his pistol. The man who had recognized Jackson went for his own piece, but for some reason it stuck as he tried to pull it free of the holster. The first bullet hit him in the shoulder, spinning him round, but the second took him fair and square in the chest, ploughing through his heart. He dropped to the ground, mortally wounded. His companion stood there, rooted to the spot and still not at all sure what was happening. By the time this man had realized that his own life was in peril, it was too late. Dave Jackson shot him down with as little compunction as he would have felt in disposing of a mad dog or injured horse.

The crashing of the gunfire was so loud that Elizabeth had clapped her hands over her ears in a vain effort out keep it out. Situated as she was, it was little short of a miracle that Jackson's horse did not trample her underfoot as it skittered sideways, spooked by the gunfire. When he was quite sure that the battle was over and the other men both dead, Jackson got down from his mount and surveyed the scene. His first instinct was to rough up the child a bit for betraying him to those others, but he knew that without her little interruption to distract the men facing him for a moment he might not have had the necessary edge to take them down. He might not beat up on her, but by God he'd make sure that she did nothing like that again, should they meet anybody on the road.

Elizabeth knew that she was in danger from this terrible man and, for want of a better strategy, she remained curled up in the dust of the road. Jackson bent down and grabbed a handful of her clothing, forcing the child to her feet. 'Come over here,' he

growled menacingly, 'I want you to see something.'
Unwillingly, with his hand still gripping the back of
her dress, she went with him to where the two
corpses sprawled on the ground. 'There, what do you
make to that?' asked Jackson. Then, before she had a
chance to reply, he gave the girl a ferocious shove,
relinquishing hold of her dress as he did so.

The sudden push made Elizabeth stumble
forward and then fall flat on her face, landing on
top of one of the dead bodies. She was to remember
the horror of that moment for the rest of her life,
waking up terrified years later as she dreamed that
she was once again that scared little girl, laying face
to face with a corpse. She began to sob hysterically
and attempted to lever herself up. In an instant,
Dave Jackson was on her, like a cat pinning down a
helpless mouse. He pressed his hand hard on her
back and said, 'Just you look there, child. See what
death looks like? Well, I'm a-telling of you now that
if'n you get cross-wise to me again, you'll end up in
the same condition.'

After having delivered himself of this threat,
Jackson gave the girl one last, hard shove, which had
the effect of causing her face to slide against that of
the dead man upon whom she was laying. Some of the
sticky blood smeared her face and she leapt to her
feet, frantically rubbing at her face in an effort to
remove the blood. Dave Jackson watched this performance with something approaching satisfaction and

said, 'Yes, I should just about say you got the message now!'

Before leaving the scene of his latest murder, Jackson spent a little time looking through the cart. There was nothing much there worth having, just a lot of household goods and suchlike. There was a satchel of food though, which he appropriated. 'Reckon they was traders,' he said. 'Most like heading to the territories too, like us.'

'What's it like there?' asked Elizabeth, having calmed down somewhat and removed all trace of the dead man's blood from her face and neck.

Dave Jackson appeared surprised to have such a civil and matter-of-fact question directed towards him and he considered carefully for a few seconds before answering. 'It's a bit different from these here parts,' he said at last. 'You won't find many white folk there, for a start. Those that are there, well, they're mostly bad lots. Road agents, boys on the scout and so on.'

'Will we be safe there?'

'Depends what you mean by safe. I ain't about to let anybody harm you or take you away, if that's what you mean. I reckon as you know after what lately happened as I can pretty well look after me and those with me.'

'What's going to happen to me when we get there?'

The question was asked in such a wistful and

artless way that for the briefest moment what passed for a heart in Dave Jackson was touched and he felt as though he was on the wrong track entirely. He looked at the little girl and recalled his own sister, many years ago. Then he remembered what a crack he was caught in and knew that only the sale of this pretty child would make it possible for him to move on and start anew elsewhere. He said briskly, 'My old grandmama, she used to say to me, "Dave, don't you ride to meet trouble halfway." I should think that about fits this present situation. For now, you got me to take care o' you and provide for your needs. When we get to the Indian Nations, why we'll have to see what chances. For now though, we're both of us fed and watered and we'll do well enough.' And with that, the girl had to be contented.

They rode on at a fairly fast trot for the rest of the day, with occasional bursts of cantering. Every once in a while Jackson would stop so that they could stretch their legs and answer any call of nature that was pressing. The killing of the two men on the road had not really affected him to any great degree. He had killed before and doubtless would again if the events demanded. Not being a religious man, he had no particular fear of murder in the abstract, as a mortal sin. His anxieties centred purely and simply around the temporal punishment that such actions often brought down upon the head of those who perpetrated them; which is as much as to say that he feared being hanged for his crimes in this world, rather than facing a reckoning in the next.

As the afternoon drew on, they found themselves riding through a pinewood that covered the lower slopes of a range of hills. It was gloomy in the wood and had she been there alone Elizabeth might have been frightened. She thought about this and then, despite the awful circumstances in which she was trapped, her lips twitched slightly and she all but smiled. It was the idea that she felt safer as a result of being in the company of this man that struck her as absurd. But then again, it made perfect sense in a way. Were she to be alone in this dark forest, then she'd be imagining all manner of dangers and not knowing whether wolves or bears, Indians or outlaws were coming through the trees to do her harm. Now though, she was tolerably sure that she need not fear anything of that sort; if nothing else, the man she was travelling with had shown himself more than capable of handling matters in a forthright and determined way. For whatever wicked reasons of his own and no matter what his ultimate plans were, Elizabeth sensed that Dave Jackson would do her no harm his self and so she was, in a strange way, safe with him. A regular baby she might have been, but Elizabeth was still old enough to find the idea a curious one and although she had never actually heard the word 'ironic' in her

119

life, she was overcome by the irony of this situation; that she felt safe because she was in the company of a dangerous killer.

CHAPTER 7

The interior of the tent smelt strange and a little musty to Zachariah, but he felt that it would be impolite to wrinkle his nose or make any outward display of what he was feeling. He suffered his grandmother to lead him to a mat, where he sat cross-legged, there being nothing in the way of furniture. When he was comfortably settled, the strange-looking woman sat opposite him and said, 'Now tell me what's afoot. Here, you can eat while you talk.' She handed him some strips of dried meat that were as hard as wood. He gave her a brief account of the events of the last few days. When he had finished, she said, 'That's the hell of a thing for a boy your age to have to endure. How old are you, son?'

'Be fifteen next birthday.'

'So your pa is dead, hey? Well, I didn't get on with him none too well and that's a fact, but still and all, I'm sorry to hear he's dead. You maybe know that's why I've had no dealings with you or my daughter these dozen years or more?'

'Ma said something.'

'So you think that your sister's been stole away by this rancher, hey? Sounds like enough. Those devils want all the land for themselves, curse them. They've been the bane of our life as well, meaning my kin here. I can't say as I'll be sorry to see us give one of 'em a bloody nose.' She gave a sudden bark of laughter and then, to Zac's astonishment, fumbled around until she came up with a short pipe, which she then proceeded to fill and light with a flint and steel.

It had been disturbing enough to hear a lady use such words as 'hell' and 'bloody' and listening to her talk of cursing folk, but in all his life Zachariah had never heard of a woman smoking. His pa had regarded the habit as being sinful and self-indulgent, but to see his own mother's mother partaking of tobacco was an almost incredible sight. She caught his look and said tartly, 'We've different customs here, boy, and you'll have to make the best of them.'

It took a little more than an hour for the warriors to be mustered, and had it not involved a close relation of Chief Tamela Pashme himself it is doubtful if it would have happened at all. The fighting between the US army and the Sioux was only now grinding to a halt and there was no appetite for any further conflict. It was already becoming clear to everybody in the tribe that the army were quite determined to seize all the Black Hills because they contained large quantities of the gold that white men so coveted. An armed band riding out of the reservation at this delicate time could bring catastrophe upon their heads and make the eventual peace treaty that they would soon have to put their names to even more onerous and unjust.

Family though was family, and when, as in this instance, the family of the chief himself was concerned, there could be no discussion. Besides which, they all loved Alice James, who had been born and raised among them many years ago. If somebody had taken her granddaughter it was a sacred duty to recover the girl at all costs.

Zachariah had not thought about it over-much, but he had rather assumed that his own role in the affair would be limited to directing the braves on the path to the McDonalds' ranch and then perhaps remaining in their village until they brought back his sister. The Indians though had quite another view of things and took it for granted that the youngster would wish to ride with them to exact vengeance upon the men who had attacked his family. That his father had been killed in this feud made it certain, from the perspective of the Santee Sioux, that the dead man's son would wish to wash his hands in the blood of the man who had committed the murder. It was unthinkable that any young man would behave otherwise.

123

None of this was stated outright, but it was fairly clear from the preparations being made that they expected Zachariah to ride along with them. This too was the expectation of his grandmother, who had spent her formative years among the Indians and, after a few years among white folk, had now lived in a tepee for so long that she saw things in just the same light as any Sioux. While the men were tacking up a pony for Zac, his grandmother said, 'What gun do you favour, boy?'

'I've only used a scattergun. For hunting, you know.'

'I think we can lay hands on such a one. Might not be the most fancy thing in the world, but it'll answer for the purpose.'

Before Zac left with the other braves, his grandmother had indeed succeeded in tracking down an exceedingly ancient duck gun, which looked as though it might have belonged to George Washington. The stock was carved walnut and the barrel chased with various floral designs, inlaid here and there with traces of gold leaf. The hammers were in the shape of dolphins. Old though it was, Zachariah was enchanted with the weapon. 'Can I really take this with me?' he asked.

'Sure you can. Here's a flask o' powder and so on to go with it.'

His grandmother had a most curious way of talking. She sounded, if not exactly like a foreigner,

124

then certainly like a person who was not used to speaking English. This was, Zac supposed, not surprising if she had spent most of her life living with Indians. Before he went off to mount up and join the troop of men heading off to track down his sister, his grandmother's brother came across to speak privately to Zachariah. Straight away, young as he was, Zac could see that this man was a different kettle of fish entirely from his sister.

Tamela Pashme or Dull Knife, chief of the Santee Sioux, did not look as though there was anything other than Indian blood flowing through his veins. His skin was as dark as any of the other Indians and his hair, except where it was streaked with iron grey, was as lustrously black as any of the tribe. Here, at least to Zachariah's untutored eye, was a real Indian. He could not guess just from looking at the man how old he was, but guessed that he and his sister must both be something above fifty years of age. Most white people of that age were already looking old, but there was no feeling, when looking at the chief of the Santee Sioux, that here was a man who would be sitting on a porch in a rocking chair any time soon! He looked every bit as capable and tough as any of his young braves.

'You are Melanie's boy,' said the chief, speaking slowly and with a much stronger accent than Zachariah's grandmother. 'My men will help you.'

This was not at all what Zac had had in mind when

he had set out seeking the help of the Indians. He had thought that they would race off and sort matters out, without his having to do anything in particular. This was not seemingly how matters stood. The Indians would help, but it was expected that he would undertake the rescue of his sister himself, which was a daunting prospect. Some of this might have shown in his face because Tamela Pashme reached out his hand and laid it on Zac's shoulder, saying, 'All men must fight for what is theirs.'

Then there was no more time to consider things deeply for the twenty warriors were mounted up and waiting for him. Zachariah slung the fowling piece over his back and went to the piebald pony that had been allotted to him. The stirrups were made of a piece of twisted rope, which was new to Zac's experience, but he managed to mount without too much difficulty. He was a tolerable fair horseman and felt that at least he would not disgrace himself in this aspect of things.

Then they were off, trotting out of the village with the women and children watching their departure as though this was a matter of great moment, which in a sense it was. It was not generally known to everybody that the great Sioux Uprising had finally petered out and some of those watching this band of braves thought that they might be off to fight the bluecoats. The presence of a young white boy did nothing to dispel this suspicion, it being no secret that their chief had white relatives.

This leaving of the Indian camp was a moment that Zachariah Hogan remembered his whole life long. He had grown up in a dingy city, as the insignificant son of a working man. Then for the last few years he had been slaving away on a patch of barren and infertile land in a remote and inhospitable area. Now though, he was somebody of consequence. Sitting on that pony, in the company of a number of fierce young warriors, with the women and children staring admiringly, why, this was being alive! This was what it felt like to be a man.

The first that either of the McDonalds knew of Melanie Hogan's presence was when she marched up behind Andrew, who was fussing and moaning with the pain of the injury to his backside, grabbed his arm from behind and then pressed a razor-sharp knife to the side of his neck. 'What say I cut your throat, you mangy dog?' she said in a hard, tight voice. 'Where's my daughter?'

McDonald, already in fear of his life from the injury that he had received, yelped as though he were in truth a dog and tried to break free. Melanie's grip was immovable though and he might as well have tried to shift an oak tree. She pressed the cold steel so hard against his throat that Andrew McDonald was in fear that she would slice into his jugular vein by accident. He squealed, 'She's not here. Before God, I don't know what's become of her.'

In earnest of her intentions and to indicate that now was not the time to be fooling around and trying to mislead her, Melanie drew the knife along the skin of the frightened man's neck, cutting through it painfully. In truth, it hurt no more than a cut taken while shaving, but for a moment Andrew McDonald genuinely believed that this madwoman had cut his throat. So great was his terror that McDonald felt his bladder loosen and realized that he was pissing down his leg. Such was the pain he was in and because of his very real fear of imminent death, he did not even care about the indignity of the thing. He just prayed that he would come out of this alive.

Josephine McDonald said, 'For God's sake spare him. Your girl ain't here, but I own we took her.'

'Not here? Where have you sent her?'

'We've sent her nowhere. Somebody took her away. I'm more sorry than I can tell. Please let my husband free.'

'I don't think so,' replied Melanie, 'Not 'til I've fathomed this out. You took her to try and steal the gold up on the bluff, isn't that right?'

'Yes, yes and it was wrong of us,' said McDonald's wife, 'We were plumb desperate and it was all we could think of.'

'You killed my husband, too.'

'Not a-purpose, I swear it. Look how he's bleeding

128

there. For mercy's sake, let me tend to him.'

Hearing confirmation that she was right and that these wretches had contrived at both the death of her husband and the abduction of her daughter, hardened Melanie Hogan's heart and she found that she was perfectly indifferent to the prospect of Andrew McDonald's death from loss of blood. She said, 'How d'ye mean, my husband wasn't killed on purpose? Speak plainly.'

Haltingly and with many an anxious glance at her husband's pants, which were now soaked with urine at the front and a good deal of blood at the rear, Josephine McDonald gave a succinct account of the events that had led to the present pass. Melanie listened attentively and when she had heard the full story exclaimed contemptuously, 'Well you're a nice set o' folks and I don't think! I never heard the like. You found yourselves in a hole and thought you'd cheat us to get out of it? And now the best man whoever walked the earth is dead and my daughter in deadly danger? I ought to kill the pair of you.'

There was nothing to be done, for this enraged woman held all the cards and it was left to both the McDonalds to stand helplessly, waiting to see what would happen to them. And all the while, Andrew McDonald was bleeding like a stuck hog and it looked to his wife as though if he did not receive some medical care presently, he was likely to expire on the spot.

129

After mulling the situation over for a minute or so, Melanie said, 'Where's your men? They expected back any time soon?'

'No,' said Josephine, 'They're out on the range. They're not apt to be back before nightfall.'

'That the truth, or are you aiming to mislead me and play for time?'

'There *is* no time,' said Josephine with great and unfeigned emotion, 'Only delay a little longer and my husband's going to bleed to death.'

'You any idea which way this man who took my child might have made off?'

'Not the least. Please, for the love of God, let me tend my husband.'

'We'll go in the house,' ordered Melanie. 'Some friends of mine will be coming by presently and they may want to speak to you folks. No tricks though, like grabbing up guns or such, you understand me?'

'Yes, yes. Please hurry.'

Beyond moaning and making noises suggestive of suffering and fear, Andrew McDonald had contributed nothing to the exchange. He was in very real fear of his life, not just from bleeding to death from the wound in his buttock, but also and more immediately from the angry woman who had a knife at his throat. He honestly did not know, and neither did Melanie Hogan, whether or not she was really planning to carve him up. It came as an immense relief therefore to learn that they were going into the house, where his wife could tend to his injury.

Still gripping McDonald's arm and holding her knife to his neck, Melanie guided her captive to move forward in the direction of the ranch house. Josephine she told to lead the way, because she did not trust either of them and was not minded to allow any room for trickery. When they entered the kitchen, Melanie gave Andrew McDonald a shove that sent him flat on his face on the tiled floor. She said to Josephine, 'You do what you will for him. You have any guns in the house? Don't lie, I know you're bound to have weaponry hid away somewhere.'

'There's a closet over yonder where my husband keeps his weapons. The key's hanging there on the wall.'

Josephine McDonald began looking to her husband's wounds by removing his pants. Since this proceeding was of what one call a private nature, and since there seemed to be no sign of treachery on the part of either husband or wife, Melanie decided to leave them to it. She went over and collected the key to the walk-in closet and took a good look around. There were various muskets, which appeared to be evenly divided between fairly up-to-date rifles and scatterguns of the sort used for hunting. There were a few handguns too, as well as boxes of ammunition and a cask of powder. Melanie chose a shiny-looking new carbine and broke open a box of bright, brass cartridges for it, to check that they fitted and were the correct ammunition. Having done so, she loaded the rifle and went back into the kitchen, where Josephine McDonald was boiling up a pan of water with a view to washing her husband's backside and cleaning the wound.

Although her heart was pounding with fear about what might have happened to Elizabeth, Melanie knew that there would be no point in rushing off to hunt for her daughter. As long as Zachariah had been able to find the village, then her mother would ensure that he received assistance. With a little good fortune, aid should arrive in a couple of hours. There was little to be done until then. That being so, Melanie remembered that she had not yet eaten that day and so, with the carbine tucked under her arm, began to prowl around the kitchen, looking for food. She found some eggs and set a pan on the range. After scooping a knob of butter into it and allowing time for the fat to start sizzling, she cracked three eggs into the pan and fried them. Josephine muttered, as she sponged down her husband's buttock, which had been fairly well sliced open by the arrow that Melanie had let fly, 'Yes, make yourself at home, why not?'

'You shut your mouth,' responded Melanie at once. 'I've consented to allow that worthless fellow to live and that's much, considering what ruin he's brought upon me and mine. I'd say that a few eggs isn't too much to take in the way of recompense.'

This was undeniably so and Josephine said nothing further.

In spite of all that had happened to him over the last few days, Zachariah was a healthy young fellow and could not help but find it exhilarating to be riding along with a company of Sioux warriors. It was the stuff of dime novels, every boy's idea of adventure. He sneaked a sideways glance at the man next to him, who was some kind of cousin. Even after racking his brains, Zac was unable to calculate just exactly what the relationship was between the two of them. This young man was the grandson of Zachariah's mother's uncle. What that made him to Zac was a mystery. Still, he was companionable enough, if a mite condescending at times. Although only three or four years older than Zac, this boy had, from what he said, already taken part in a real war.

The Santee Sioux had sent forces to join in the fighting against the soldiers who were, as it seemed to them, trying to help the prospectors desecrate the holy land of the Black Hills, but this had been done on a more or less unofficial basis. The Lakota and the Sioux tribes under Sitting Bull's leadership were in open rebellion and had left the reservations to fight the army. Tamela Pashme's tribe, on the other hand, had stayed put in Pine Ridge, but the chief had turned a blind eye to individuals who wanted to go and join the uprising. One of these hotheads had been his own grandson, who was now helping mount the mission to rescue Elizabeth Hogan.

Zachariah had taken to Ochtheli, as he had given his name to be, because for one thing he spoke good enough English that it was possible to hold a conversation with him. As for most of the other braves, it was not easy to gauge just precisely how much they did and didn't understand. Zachariah addressed remarks to some of them in an effort to be sociable, but they just smiled or said 'Yes' in response. He wondered if they were secretly annoyed to be sent off like this to help recover some little white girl they knew nothing about.

It was a beautiful day though and in spite of all the misfortunes that had fallen upon him, Zachariah was a normal boy, which mean that even the worst tragedy was not likely to maintain its hold on him for all that long. The novelty of being in the company of a bunch of Indians was such that it served to drive from his mind all thoughts about the recent death of his father. It wasn't that Zac was an especially heartless or callous youth, but it must be said that he had become mightily sick over the last year of digging, hoeing, watering and weeding for little or no return. Caleb Hogan might well have been, as his widow now asserted, the best man ever to walk the earth, but he was far from being an affectionate or demonstrative parent. He was a man who lived his life by the Good Book and expected no less of those around him, his own family included. This meant that both Zac and Betty were a deal closer to their mother than they had been to Caleb.

Ochtheli said, 'You are dreaming, cousin!'

'I'm sorry, I was a long way from here, leastways in spirit. What did you say?'

'I said we'll go to the ford and then you can tell us which way from there.'

'Surely. It's real good of you fellows to help us, you know. I don't know how to thank you.'

The young man riding beside him gave Zachariah an odd look. He said, 'In a manner of speaking, your family is of our tribe. We wouldn't abandon one of our own, not ever.'

'Well, I'm grateful all the same.'

Then, to Zac's surprise and embarrassment, Ochtheli asked, 'What do you want us to do when we cross the Niobrara?'

The idea that he was in some way in charge of the expedition was more than Zachariah could comprehend. He felt that he was more or less tagging along in the group and now this man was asking what they should do! He said, 'My ma was sure that this big rancher, man called McDonald, has taken Betty. I should think we ought to head for his place first.'

Ochtheli thought this over and then said, 'You don't mind fighting against your own people?'

'I don't rightly understand you,' said Zac, 'What do you mean by fighting against my own people?'

Again, the other man shot him a strange look. Then he said, 'If we ride down on this ranch and there are men there, white men, then we'll have to fight them. They won't let us come and search the place. Are you ready to fight white men along with us?'

Strange to relate, Zachariah Hogan had not hitherto given any thought to the actual mechanics of taking back his baby sister from a powerful rancher. Somehow he had simply assumed that they would turn up at the ranch and that would be that. He said haltingly, 'Well you know, family is family. If my little sister is at that ranch, why then I hope they'll just hand her over, peaceable like. If not, then it'll be on the heads of them as try to stop us, I reckon. I ain't lookin' for trouble, but if they want it then I guess I can oblige all right.'

Ochtheli merely nodded soberly at this brief statement, but inwardly, he rejoiced. When first he had met this youngster, the boy had had the air of a beggar, seeking alms. Now though, he was growing before Ochtheli's very eyes, into a young warrior. This was a marvellous thing to behold after only such a short length of time. Perhaps talking to the chief's sister had effected this change or, more likely, it was the Sioux blood in him coming to the fore. Whatever the reason though, Ochtheli was greatly looking forward to seeing with his own eyes a boy turning into a man.

It had passed midday, of that Melanie was sure. She said, 'Is there a clock in this place?'

'There's one through there, in the other room,' replied Josephine McAndrew. After cleaning the wound, she had pressed a clean rag over the cut on her husband's buttock and bound it in place with a length of material obtained by ripping up an old shirt that was stowed in a drawer. Having done this, she had asked Melanie's permission to fetch a clean pair of pants from another part of the house. It had been on the tip of Melanie Hogan's tongue to say that the injured man could just make do with the sodden garment that he had been wearing, but then she felt that this was cruel and petty. She had let his wife go off, but not before reminding her that she was holding a loaded and cocked carbine and that if there was any funny business then she would not hesitate to open fire.

After checking the clock, Melanie found that it still lacked a few minutes to noon. How time was dragging! She calculated that if her son had ridden straight to the village of the Santee Sioux and they had agreed with no further ado to send aid then they would most likely be here by around one, two at the latest. After cross-questioning Josephine McDonald, she had figured that Betty must have been taken at about eight in the morning. That meant that this

Jackson, assuming that that was who had taken her, had a good four-hour start on any pursuers.

Because she was restless and fidgety and for want of anything else to pass the time, Melanie said, 'I should think that you two have pretty much all you could want here. Why'd you have to try and steal what we had as well?'

Andrew McDonald, who now that he did not have a knife pressing against his throat seemed to have recovered some of his natural vigour, began explaining about their problems. His wife chipped in from time to time and within ten minutes the two of them had spelled out the whole circumstances surrounding the death of Melanie's husband and the carrying off of her child. After hearing all that they had to say, Melanie did not speak for fully half a minute and then shook her head and opined, 'That's the hell of a tale. Assuming of course that it's a true bill.'

'It's true enough,' said Josephine. 'You think I'd get up to such tricks if I weren't desperate?'

'Other folk get into such scrapes, without any killing and child-stealing,' said Melanie. 'Don't even try and make out as you had no choice in the matter or was forced into it.'

Neither Josephine nor her husband could think of an adequate reply to this and so remained silent.

Elizabeth grasped the front of the saddle to balance herself, but from time to time she swayed and came close to falling from the horse. When this happened, Dave Jackson would take one hand from the reins and steady her. As they moved through the dark wood, Elizabeth asked suddenly, 'How long will it take us to get where we're going?'

Jackson, who was by natural disposition a chatty and talkative man and had been finding the protracted silences wearisome, was pleased to have something to talk about. He said, 'I guess that depends. If we go on at this pace, it could be four or five days. A little more fast riding and we might trim it down to three.'

'Do you have a home?'

'A home? You mean, like a house where I live or something? No, not at all. I go where I will.'

'Don't you get lonely?'

'I'm not a perfect fool. Start feeling like that and afore you know it, you're trapped.'

The child's question had touched something in Dave Jackson's heart, for the fact was that he hadn't had any sort of home, in the sense of a permanent base, since he was knee-high to a grasshopper. The little girl's words worked within him, like yeast, and after a few minutes he began to feel a little sad. That passed soon enough though and he was possessed by a great and inarticulate irritation against Elizabeth for leading his thoughts in such a direction. He said, 'You think you're right smart, but you ain't. You'll see. Home, indeed!'

Now the fact was that Dave Jackson was by this time fearfully tired and desired nothing so much as to snatch a few winks of sleep. This was making him even sharper than usual. They were, he thought, far enough from both the McDonalds' ranch and the farmhouse that he had robbed to make pursuit a fairly unlikely eventuality and, all else being equal, he could afford a little rest before they continued journeying on until nightfall. The only thing was, what was he to do with this wretched child? Wouldn't she try and flee while he slumbered?

It does not seem possible that any human being would think of doing such a thing, but the idea that Jackson came up with was that he would hog-tie the little girl, as though she were an animal, and that he would then be able to sleep in peace, knowing that she was unable to escape. He had a length of rope in his saddle-bag that would be the very thing for such a job. They would have to get off the track though, so that no passing busybody should wonder why a young girl was trussed up in that way. Jackson guided his horse to the right and began weaving a way through the fir trees. Elizabeth said, 'Why have we left the road?'

'Because I'm dog-tired and need some sleep,' replied Jackson shortly, 'I guess you could do with a rest too after travelling like this for so long.'

When they reached what Jackson conceived to be a convenient spot, a little clearing in the forest, he

140

halted and dismounted. Then he rummaged around at the back of the saddle until he had found the rope. He said to Elizabeth, 'I can't take any chances with you, not since that performance back there when you nearly got me shot. I'm going to have to make sure that you don't run away, you know.'

'You don't have to do that,' said the child, scared at the sight of the rope, 'I'll give you my oath.'

'Well it ain't what you'd call enough. Now turn round, so I can bind your hands.'

After tying the girl's hands behind her back, not tightly, but most efficiently, Jackson ran the rope down and lashed her ankles together with no more emotion than if he had been doing the same to a dumb animal. Then he checked the knots and said, 'I reckon that'll do. I'm going to rest now and I'd advise you to do the same.'

After securing his horse, Dave Jackson lay down upon the ground and almost immediately fell into a deep and dreamless sleep. As for Elizabeth Hogan, she wriggled over to a tree and sat upright, leaning against it. How this was to be resolved, she had no ideas at all.

CHAPTER 8

When Zachariah first met up with the Indians, they had been armed only with the traditional weapons of their people: knives, clubs, bows and arrows and lances. Now though, they all seemed to be sporting various guns, including very up-to-date-looking cavalry carbines. It struck Zac that these might well have been looted from some battlefield such as Little Bighorn. This was a most alarming thought. It was while he was turning over in his mind how he felt about riding shoulder to shoulder with some of those who might have been involved in the massacre of Custer and his men that he realized that something was going on.

Some of the men were looking across to their left and making terse, monosyllabic comments, which of course Zac did not understand. He stared beyond them and saw that there was another party of horsemen, keeping pace with them. He said to Ochtheli,

'Is something wrong?'

'It is with those others to say,' said the young man calmly, 'We have our business and they have theirs. If they do not trouble us, all will be well.'

But the other riders, a smaller party than their own, evidently did wish to trouble them, for they changed course and began heading in their direction. In fact, they were cowboys, employed by Andrew McDonald. Seeing a bunch of Indians who were not in their proper place, that is to say on the reservation, these fellows had taken it upon themselves to investigate and perhaps send the savages back to where they belonged. They were young men, braggarts and hotheads, who had persuaded themselves that it was their duty to tend to this incursion into their own district.

To Zachariah's consternation, some of those with whom he was riding began unslinging rifles and drawing pistols. They were seemingly quite prepared to give the seven or eight white men whatever they wished. Perhaps the cowboys didn't grasp the significance of this or thought that they could bluff the others into turning aside, because they began whooping and shouting as though they were rounding up cattle. It was all a game to them and they were thinking about how they would be able to tell the patrons of the saloon in Benton's Crossing the coming Saturday night how they had single-handedly prevented an Indian attack on their town. It was not to be.

143

The cowboys rode slightly ahead of the other riders, presumably trying to head them off. When they were fifty yards away, a couple of the Sioux began shooting, without any warnings or other preliminary actions. Zac had vaguely thought that a confrontation of this kind would follow roughly the same course as a tussle between boys in the schoolyard. First would come threats and warlike cries, then first one party and then the other would withdraw and only after such a ritual would any fighting commence. This was not at all how the Indian warriors played it. These men were coming close enough to represent a danger and that was sufficient in itself to be the signal for bloodshed. As he watched, two of the white men tumbled from their horses. One fell clear, but the other had a foot tangled still in one stirrup and he was dragged and bounced along behind his panicking horse. It was a terrible thing to behold.

In addition to the two men, a horse had also been hit and this stumbled along for a bit before collapsing into a heap and throwing its rider. All this was obviously a lot more than the group of young cowboys had bargained for. The response to their crowding had been so sudden and lethal that they must have seen that to continue along their present course would like enough end in the death of them all. They were tough enough when dealing with dumb beasts, but coming up against a band of determined and ruthless warriors was more dangerous

144

than they could ever have imagined. The survivors veered off and withdrew to a safe distance, slowing down and then stopping. There were no casualties among the Sioux. Ochtheli gave a cry of sheer, exuberant delight and said in a loud voice to Zac, 'They didn't know who they were dealing with!'

As they rode on towards the McDonalds' place, Zachariah was filled with a sudden foreboding. These men would stick at naught, killing their fellow-beings as casually as he would shoot down a jack-rabbit. Had his ma called upon more than she had known? Then it struck the youngster that, having lived with these folk for years, she would probably have known just exactly what she was doing. She did not intend for whoever had meddled with her daughter to live to the end of his natural span.

Andrew McDonald was looking pale and anxious, for the arrow wound had still not stopped bleeding. The dressing that his wife had affixed to his backside was now sodden through and the clean pants he had on were already saturated with blood. Josephine said to Melanie Hogan, 'My husband needs a doctor. He's like to die, else.'

Melanie shrugged and said indifferently, 'When my friends come, we'll be leaving and you and he can do as you will. Until then you just set there, where I can keep a watch on you.'

'Ain't you got a human heart?'

'I wonder you dare ask that of me,' said Melanie, turning to stare at the other woman with pitiless and cold eyes. 'You start down the road o' stealing away folks' children, this is the reward you reap.' Josephine McDonald was about to reply, but Melanie said, 'Hush, now. I hear riders.'

The troop of Indians thundered into the yard outside the McDonalds' house. Zachariah had thought that this would be the best place to begin the search for his sister; after all, Ma was sure that these were the folks who had spirited her away. He was overjoyed when his mother emerged from the house, although slightly disconcerted to see that she was clutching a rifle. Then a very strange thing happened. Melanie Hogan went up to one of the Indians and began speaking rapidly in what he supposed must be Sioux. His mother had never said anything about learning the Indian language, but now he considered, it made sense if she had indeed lived among them for two years. When she had finished, she came over to Zac and said, 'Well, you managed all right, son. A couple of these here fellows'll scout around now and look for the trail of a lone man on horseback. Your sister's not here.'

It took little time for the men to return and report that somebody had laid for hours in the little spinney overlooking the house. There were further signs that a man bearing a heavy burden had stumbled up the slope to the little rise and that he had then ridden off

146

east. Zachariah, who had not even dismounted, leaned down from the saddle so that his ma could kiss him. She said, 'Ride well and be sure to bring back your sister safe and sound.'

After the Indians and her son had departed, Melanie went back into the kitchen of the McDonalds' house and said, 'I'll be leaving now. You two can do as you please.'

'Thank the Lord,' said Josephine McDonald, casting an anxious glance at her husband, who was sitting crookedly in a chair and still bleeding heavily, 'Andrew can't ride, not in that condition. Will you lend a hand to get the buggy tacked up and ready to go?'

'No, I don't reckon so,' said Melanie in surprise. 'Why would you think it for a moment?'

'I'm begging you. Please, as one woman to another. I don't know if I can do it alone.'

Melanie shrugged and said, 'It's no affair of mine.' Then she gathered up her bow and arrows, ejected the shells from the carbine and laid it on the table. Before she left, she said, 'You and that man have wrought nothing but evil for me and mine. It's enough that I'm leaving you with your lives. You tell a soul of what happened to yon scoundrel and I guess folk'll be asking about my husband's killing and my daughter. Far as I'm concerned, we're through.' She walked to the door and then turned and delivered herself of a few parting words. 'Unless of course, anything bad has befallen my little girl. In which case, I'll be back here to kill the pair of you.' Then she was gone.

It was something of a mystery to Zachariah just how the Indians could tell who had passed where and even what weight the rider had been, but they were seemingly able to do so. If they said that the man who had most likely taken Elizabeth had travelled east along the track, then he for one was perfectly prepared to take their word for it.

Ochtheli was, for an Indian, a lively and talkative kind of fellow. After they had left the McDonalds' ranch, he said to Zac, 'Your mother speaks our language like an Indian.'

'She said she lived with you people for some time. When she was child, you know.'

'Yes. I met her once before, you know. When I was very small. She came to visit her mother.'

'Yes, she told me.'

'She isn't one I would want to cross with.'

'No, I guess not.'

The weather was still beautifully fine and if the purpose of the expedition had not been so grim, then Zachariah would have enjoyed a ride out along a road he'd not been down before. As it was though, he kept thinking about those men who had tried to tangle with the Indians and shivered at how readily the Sioux had just shot them down. It dawned on him that these men had almost certainly been mixed up in the war with the army last year and were ready and willing to kill anybody who got in their way or threatened them. He was wondering uneasily what would happen when they caught up with this man who had rode off with Betty. Would they kill him too or, which was even worse, expect him to kill the man?

A good enough horseman he might have been, but the pace set by the Indians was a punishing one. They said that the horse they were tracking had moved mostly at a trot, but sometimes at a canter. That meant that if they wished to overtake it before dusk they must maintain a steady canter for almost the whole of the time. Their hardy ponies were equal to the task and showed no signs of flagging, even after two hours of more or less continuous cantering, with brief spells of trotting to enable them to catch their breath. Zachariah's seat was starting to feel a little sore when they came in sight of a small forest, through which the road went. They reined in before entering the woods. Ochtheli said, 'This would be a good place for an ambush. We'll slow down and set the horses walking. Don't want to let all the world know that we're coming.'

The track was covered in a thick layer of brown needles from the pines and that, combined with the fact that they were only proceeding at a walk, meant that the whole place was eerily quiet. It was a sharp contrast to the rhythm of rapid hoof-beats that had

so far marked their progress across the open country.
Later on, Zac had to think carefully to put the events
in their right order, because when a lot of things
happen one after another, especially in unfamiliar
surroundings, there is a tendency to get them all
jumbled up in your mind when remembering what
has occurred.

They were almost out of the wood and could see
the road stretching out ahead of them towards some
undulating grassland, when a faint sound reached
their ears. It was the brassy and altogether unmis-
takeable sound of a bugle call. One of the men called
over to Ochtheli, who shouted something back.
Then, as clear as could be, Zachariah heard his
sister's voice shouting, 'Help! Somebody help me!'
And at just the moment that he knew that his sister
was alive, nearby and in need of his assistance, Zac
saw a troop of blue-coated cavalry appear on the crest
of a low hill that the road led to, something less than
a mile away. He had already begun to dismount, but
seeing the cavalry he wondered if he should remain
with the warriors and not desert them.

Ochtheli's eyes were shining and he said, 'That
was your sister, no? Go, then. We will deal with this.'
When Zac looked doubtful, the Sioux said, 'Hurry
now, your time is upon you.' Ever afterwards, the boy
was to recollect those words and years later dated the
onset of his manhood to that moment. He jumped
down and cocked both hammers of the scattergun

that his grandmother had given him. Then he made his way cautiously through the trees to where his sister's voice had come from.

It was shadowy and dark, but up ahead Zac could see some movement. He moved forward carefully, peering to see what was going on. It looked to him as though two people were struggling and then he heard a child cry out in distress. Abandoning caution, he ran forward, holding his weapon at high port, and found himself in a clearing. His sister was being manhandled by an ill-favoured fellow who was holding her upright with one hand and slapping her with the other. Zachariah lifted the gun to his shoulder and shouted as loud as he could, 'Hey you! Just let her alone, you hear what I tell you?' And no sooner had he spoken the words when there came the sound of gunfire behind him, combined with confused shouting and the thudding of hoofs. He guessed that the soldiers had reached his friends.

Dave Jackson had been sound asleep when he was awoken by Elizabeth calling for help. She had heard voices from the road and figured that this was the best chance she would get to escape from this awful man. She shouted as loud as she could. When Jackson came to and knew what was going on, he was possessed by a great fury and grabbed hold of the little girl. He lifted her up by the rope that bound her and held her against the trunk of a tree. Then he began cuffing her hard around her head. It was when

he heard the boy yelling that Dave Jackson had a pre-
monition of disaster. He turned around and found
himself staring down the twin barrels of a scattergun
held by an angry looking youth whom he calculated
was twenty feet from him.

That it was a shotgun he had to deal with and not
a rifle, worked in Jackson's favour, or so he thought.
Had it been a rifle then the young rascal might have
loosed off a shot and had a good chance of taking
Jackson and missing the girl. As things stood though,
at that range the buckshot would spread out and be
sure to take the two of them. Quick as you like,
Jackson whirled the girl around and held her in front
of him to make sure that the kid dare not fire. While
he did so, Dave Jackson could hear a regular gun
battle developing near at hand. Lord knows what was
going on, but it was certainly high time for him to be
gone from there.

'Put down your gun and I'll let her go,' said
Jackson, 'Otherwise, I swear I'll kill her.' He was
trying to hold the struggling child with one hand so
that he could use his other to draw his pistol and take
down this impudent youngster, who had the temerity
to aim a shotgun at him. Dave Jackson really didn't
take to having a shotgun pointing in his direction in
this way. The only difficulty with this plan was that
the child was now fighting tooth and nail to get free
and it was all he could do, using both hands, to keep
her positioned in front of him to shield him from

harm. Even if he could hold her with one hand, she was moving about so violently that there was no chance that he would be able to aim steadily. And all the time, he could hear the crash of gunfire from near at hand. Lord only knew what was going on.

It really seemed as though they had reached an impasse, because while the young fellow could not hazard a shot at Jackson, he for his part could not get his gun out and fire at the boy. This standoff was resolved by Elizabeth Hogan who, without any warning at all, twisted her head round and clamped her teeth on Dave Jackson's bare wrist. She bit down with as much force as she could muster and it felt to Jackson as though a dog had seized him. The shock of the unexpected pain caused him to loosen his grip and, like a young animal, Elizabeth dived free, hurling herself to the ground.

This looked like the opportunity that Dave Jackson had been waiting for and his hand snaked down to his gun as he glanced up to check where his target was. He knew though in that moment that he was not going to make it. The boy had that shotgun aiming dead at him and the eyes that glittered above the barrel, taking aim, were among the most merciless and hard that Jackson could ever recall. Instinct kept him going though and his hand had actually grasped the hilt of the revolver before the first shot took him full in the face, shredding his features beyond recognition. Almost at once, the young man lowered his aim and fired the second barrel, this time catching Jackson in the belly.

It is surprising and quite shocking, the amount of damage that can be caused to a human body by a couple of charges of buckshot, fired at close range. Jackson's head was a featureless, bloody pulp, the face having been altogether obliterated. The force of the second blast had ripped away his shirt and opened a hole in his stomach, from which part of his intestines now protruded. Elizabeth was spared this sight, for she ran at once to embrace her brother. As he clasped her in his arms though, Zachariah Hogan was mesmerized by what he saw and the terrifying knowledge that this carnage was all his work. He was holding Betty to his breast with one arm, his other hand still holding the scattergun. Sickened at what he saw, he hurled it from himself with great force and then, making sure that his sister did not catch so much as a glimpse of the awful vision that had seared itself onto his memory, he led her away from the scene, after first untying the knots that held her.

'What about his horse?' asked Elizabeth. 'It's tethered over there.'

They went over and freed the horse. Zac noticed that the shooting seemed to have stopped now and there was only the sound of men's voices shouting. He said to Betty, 'Listen Sis, we got to be careful. There's some soldiers down there and if we just appear out of nowhere, maybe they'll take us for the enemy.'

As they neared the roadway, a lot of men could be seen through the trees, moving about, busily engaged in some task or other. Zac waited until they were within hailing distance, then he took his sister behind a tree and shouted at the top of his voice, 'Don't nobody shoot. Me and my little sister need help.' It was all that he could think of and at least the appeal was not met with a fusillade of fire. Instead, somebody hollered back, 'Show yourselves, but with your hands raised.'

And so Zachariah Hogan and his sister surrendered themselves to a troop of the US Cavalry who had been heading towards the reservations of Dakota to make sure that those living there were not minded to cause any further trouble, now that the Great Sioux War was officially ended. It took some time to account for their presence in the woods, but they were so young and innocent that in the end it was assumed that they could have had nothing to do with the band of Redskins who had just ambushed the column.

After the two youngsters had come down to the road, being covered warily with rifles by two suspicious troopers, an officer was called over to question them. Before he arrived, Zachariah looked round sadly. Every one of the men he had rode here with was laying dead, along with a dozen cavalrymen. He saw Ochtheli, on his back, with his eyes open and staring sightlessly up at the trees. Those men had given their lives, for what? For the cause of their tribe? Surely not for him, to give him a chance to rescue Betty? Before he had come to a satisfactory answer to this question, a young captain came up. He said, 'What the deuce are you two children doing here? Where have you come from?'

Zac said, truthfully enough, that his sister had been lost and that he had ridden in search of her and here she was. When he had finished speaking, he indicated his sister. The captain looked at her and any thought that there could be any deception or sharp dealing involved here, evaporated at once. Here was, very obviously, a frightened little girl, clinging affectionately to the young fellow who had found her. Captain Marshall said, 'Well, we're bound in the first instance for Benton's Crossing and if that's of any use to you, then you folk are very welcome to ride along of us. I see you have a mount of your own.'

Zachariah would have liked a few moments alone with the slain Indians, but felt that it would be impolitic to acknowledge that these men were anything to do with him. It was enough that the soldiers were not asking any difficult questions about how his sister had been lost and managed to find her way out here. For that he was truly grateful.

CHAPTER 9

The death of the party of Santee Sioux with whom
Zachariah Hogan had been riding was the final
chapter in the Great Sioux War. Altogether, eighteen
Indians and fourteen cavalry troopers were killed in
the engagement on the edge of that Nebraska
pinewood, and the Battle of Kennet Valley Wood in
1877 went down in history. The role played in it by
Zachariah Hogan was, however, destined to remain
unknown, for which he was, both at the time and in
later life, profoundly grateful.

Melanie Hogan's joy at the safe return of her children was unbounded. Later, she would grieve for the
loss of those men from her mother's tribe, but at first
she was selfishly pleased to have her son and daughter back home safely and be damned to how many
others had lost their lives to bring this about. The day
after Zachariah came home, his mother said to him,
'Well son, killing a man's not something you ever

157

forget, so don't bother trying. You did what you had to and a lot of folk lost their lives through it, but you did what you set out to do and that's about enough, I reckon.'

'You ever kill anybody, Ma?'

'I don't know.'

Zac looked at his mother and, shaken as he was by the events of the last few days, all but smiled. 'You don't know if you ever killed anybody? That's blazing strange!'

Melanie sketched out briefly what had taken place when she paid a visit to the McDonalds. After doing so, she concluded by saying, 'Truth to tell, I shouldn't wonder if that fellow bled to death. I think my arrow nicked some vessel and effected a mischief. Still, there it is.'

'You feel bad about it?'

'Not over-much, no. They'd no business coming here trying to cheat us and taking away your sister. To say nothing of killing your pa. No, I wouldn't be too sorrowful, were I to learn that I killed that Andrew McDonald.'

Elizabeth was still sleeping in the house and Zac and his mother were standing some yards away, near the stream, because they did not wish to wake the girl, feeling that it was good for her to sleep and forget about the awful thing that had befallen her. Zachariah looked across to the bluff and said, 'Are we staying or going, Ma?'

'I think we'd be fools to leave until we survey that rock and see what might be found there.'

The Black Hills gold rush was in full swing and in the second half of 1877 the northern part of Nebraska too became another spot where folks thought that their fortune might be made. The news of the rich lode of auriferous metal found up on what became known as Hogan's Bluff was sufficient to lure many prospectors to the area. As is generally the case, a few were lucky, but most were not. The Hogans though were assured of their fortune because the land on which they struck gold was indisputably theirs alone.

There was no question of tilling the land and Melanie and her son devoted all their energies to panning and digging. Eventually, they set up a company that built a mine on the bluff and with the profits from that became richer than anybody else thereabouts.

All this good fortune was, for Melanie, marred by one circumstance and that was that Andrew McDonald had indeed died, barely two hours after she had left the ranch house that fateful day. He'd never even made it to town because his wife feared to leave him untended while she tacked up the buggy. He had simply passed away quietly in the kitchen, where Melanie had last seen him, with his wife sitting helplessly by his side. This was not a terrible burden on Melanie Hogan's conscience, but she would rather the wretch hadn't died, no matter how richly some would say he deserved it. There it was though and whenever she felt a twinge of guilt about it, Melanie Hogan fetched out her late husband's Bible, where she saw it written as blunt as could be in the Gospel of Matthew, 'All who will take up the sword, will die by the sword.'